WINTER'S CRIMES 12

Edited by Hilary Watson

ISBN 0 333 28987 0

First published 1980 by
MACMILLAN LONDON LIMITED
4 Little Essex Street London WC2R 3LF
and Basingstoke
Associated companies in Delhi, Dublin, Hong Kong,
Johannesburg, Lagos, Melbourne, New York, Singapore
and Tokyo

Photoset in Great Britain by
ROWLAND PHOTOTYPESETTING LIMITED
Bury St Edmunds, Suffolk

Printed in Great Britain by
ST EDMUNDSBURY PRESS
Bury St Edmunds, Suffolk

Contents

Editor's Note 7

Box Number 742
    by Ted Allbeury 9

Big Boy, Little Boy
    by Simon Brett 24

Black Museum
    by Celia Dale 52

The Scribbler's Tale
    by David Fletcher 66

Audited and Found Correct
    by Michael Gilbert 86

The Winning Trick
    by Laurence Meynell 101

A Good Night's Sleep
    by Anne Morice 124

Family Butcher
    by George Sims 138

Report from Section Nine
    by Michael Sinclair 160

Finale
    by Michael Underwood 174

I Hate Kids
    by John Wainwright 192

Treasure Finds a Mistress
    by David Williams 203

EDITOR'S NOTE

Winter's Crimes 12 continues the tradition of the series by containing a collection of stories which are all new and have never before been published in Great Britain.

The twelve stories in this volume contain a variety of devious crimes and my thanks go to the distinguished contributors for their help and talents in creating such a wealth of entertainment: and my special thanks go to George Hardinge for once more enabling me to undertake such an enjoyable task.

Hilary Watson

Ted Allbeury

BOX NUMBER 742

When our switchboard girl said that a Mr Hacker wanted to speak to me I didn't recognise the name, and because I was in a meeting I asked her to check who he was and what he wanted.

The meeting dragged on and she didn't come back to me; and for some reason I didn't notice the message she had left on my desk until the following morning. It said briefly – 'Mr Hacker's call was personal. Knew you in Army. Will call again today. Angie.'

I ought to have remembered his name even after ten years, but somehow when they give you your chalk-striped suit and your brown trilby and your accumulated pay it all kind of fades away. But you've signed a piece of paper that goes on about the Official Secrets Act and they side-line Clause 2. They also require you to keep them informed of any change of address.

I'd changed addresses three times since I was de-mobbed in 1947 and I hadn't notified them of any of the changes. Maybe subconsciously it was bloody-minded and deliberate, but there's enough to remember when you're moving home without worrying about keeping MI6 informed that you've moved from Finchley to Sanderstead.

When Hacker called mid-morning his voice was friendly and persuasive. They'd like to have a word with me. It was urgent and they'd like to suggest that we met at the Grosvenor Hotel at Victoria that afternoon. And that, as Hacker pointed out, was handy for my office and handy for catching my normal 5.17 from platform 16 at Victoria Station. I took the point silently that they knew my habits, and said I'd see them at four for tea and toast.

The agency was doing a pitch for the Cunard account in two days' time and the pressures meant that I thought no more about Hacker for the rest of the morning. But my efficient secretary sent me off to my rendezvous in good time.

The lounge of the Grosvenor Hotel still has a touch of Somerset Maugham about it. Men with distinguished white hair and heavy tans signal to waiters for more hot water with gestures that are distinctly east of Suez. Although Suez was not a word to be bandied about in those summer days of 1957.

They arrived on the dot at four. Hacker and Loveridge. It was like old times except that in those days it had tended to be whisky rather than tea.

Loveridge looked much the same. Shaggy and unkempt, despite what were obviously expensive clothes. And his hair still looked as if it had been hacked at by the regimental barber. He still wore the heavy spectacles that emphasised the moon shape of his pale face. Nevertheless Arthur Loveridge could speak most Middle East languages better than the natives. The sad thing is that if you speak a foreign language perfectly you can seldom be used in the field because you stick out like a cat at Crufts against the rough demotic chat of the locals. So Loveridge was a desk man.

Hacker, like me, was somewhere in his middle thirties, and a field officer. We had both specialised in penetrating enemy underground movements, Hacker in what was then Persia and Irak, and me against the Italians from east to north Africa and eventually in Italy. We were both successful operators but our masters had never been happy with our methods. We got criticised like the Met are criticised now, for hob-nobbing with the enemy. It was a waste of time explaining the facts of life to desk-bound majors in St James's Street. We may be fighting to the death with a ruthless enemy but there were things that a British officer could never do. Unfortunately Hacker and I did them, so I never made more than major, and Hacker had to wait until I was demobbed before he got his turn. But it's an ill-wind, and Intelligence Corps pips and crowns with their green felt backing were in short supply, and I was able to sell Joe Hacker my battle-dress jacket complete with crowns. One of the main differences between us was that Hacker loved parachuting, and I hated it. Somebody in Personnel once said to me that it was a very revealing characteristic on Hacker's part. I always reckoned it had something to do with the fact that Hacker wasn't very good with girls. He was good-looking and jolly but somehow he never clicked. There was something about Joe Hacker that girls rumbled. I still don't know what it was. I asked a girl once and she looked back half-smiling and shook her head. She had a knowing look in her eyes that implied that she knew something all right but didn't want to disillusion me.

We went through the usual bits about health and wives while the waiter was setting out the tea-things and then Hacker leaned forward and tapped my knee.

'We need a bit of help, Johnny.'

'Go on.'

'You've read about the troubles in Cyprus?'

'You mean Makarios and all those acronyms – ELAS – ENOSSIS – and back to the Greek homeland stuff?'

'That's it.'

'I've never been to Cyprus, Joe, how can I help?'

'All the Greeks and Cypriots in this country have been sending out floods of cash for arms to murder our chaps who are trying to keep them from one another's throats. We've stopped all the individual money by Bank of England regulations, but the bastards have found one last dodge that we haven't been able to stop. That's where you could help.'

'Tell me.'

'They've bought up a small advertising agency and they ship the money out as payments for advertising in Cypriot newspapers. The ads never appear of course and the cash goes for buying arms.'

'And you want to stop it?'

'Yes.'

'Is it a genuine agency?'

'Yes. No big accounts, but it's legitimate all right.'

'Has it got recognition?'

'What's that?'

'Is it recognised by the Institute? It can't place ads in the UK and get proper terms for discounts without recognition.'

Hacker looked at Loveridge with raised eyebrows and Loveridge, as always, knew the answer.

'Yes, it's fully recognised.'

'What sort of turnover?'

'About six hundred thousand but a lot more if you throw in the cash going through to Cyprus.'

'How much more?'

'Twenty thousand a month more. Sometimes as much as forty.'

'Who subscribes it?'

'Every Greek and Cypriot waiter and ponce in Soho for a start.'

'In cash?'

'Yes.'

I looked at Joe Hacker. 'Why don't you just send the boys in to wreck the place. They'll take the hint.'

'They'll just find some other dodge. Apart from that the Foreign Office insist that we don't do anything that could be even vaguely made to look like harassment.

We're still holding hands with Athens to try and cool it down.'

'Does this cash make any real difference?'

'It makes a lot of difference. It's about half of what they get from all sources.'

'What do you want me to do?'

'We want you to come up with some idea that stops this bloody agency playing games without it being connected in any way with the Foreign Office or the security services.'

'Any ideas?'

'None. That's why we're talking to you.'

'How long have we got?'

'We want to clobber them as quickly as possible. A couple of months at the outside.'

'OK. I'll phone you tomorrow.'

We spent about fifteen minutes gossiping about our old friends and what they were doing in civilian life. The nice guys were on the bread-line teaching in secondary schools, and the real bastards had Ferarris and Rolls Royces, living high off immoral earnings or running arms and drugs in fast boats across the Med.

By the time I'd got to Sanderstead I had the first glimmerings of a possible way of dealing with our advertising friends. I slept on it and it still looked a runner next morning but it had some holes in it.

Barnes Advertising Agency Limited was in Lower Belgrave Street and had been established for ten years. The two directors had sold out a year ago but had been kept on to run the place, the legitimate part that is. They probably didn't even know about the fun and games that the new owners were up to.

There were four directors. The two original owners, both English, George Parker and Arthur Matins. And the two new owners, Panayotis Pattakos and Nicolas Sinodynos. At least those were the names on the registration at Companies House.

I phoned Hacker and arranged another meeting at the Grosvenor. Both of them came, and Hacker was obviously pleased that I had come back so quickly.

'What resources have we got, Joe?'

'What do you mean – money or people?'

'Both.'

'Very little money and no people. Are you expecting to make anything out of it?'

'Yes.'

His eyes were amused, and beady, and envious.

'How much?'

'Not money, just a favour.'

'Go on.'

'Get my agency one of the government advertising accounts. The Army recruiting campaign or short-service commissions. Something like that.'

'I haven't got that much influence.'

'I know. But your bosses have.'

He didn't like the dig but he nodded.

'I'll see what I can do.'

'Have you got any contacts in Tangier?'

'We've got an office there.'

'Any bods?'

'One from London and two locals.'

'Reliable?'

'Enough.'

'Who's in charge of Photographic now?'

'It's still Hamish McKay.'

'Can I borrow him?'

'How long for?'

'A couple of days.'

'That would be OK.'

'What's the money budget?'

He half-smiled. 'Tell me what you need.'

'About a thousand quid. Maybe you'll get some change or maybe I'll need a bit more.'

'What's the plan?'

'You'd best not know, sweetheart. Just leave it to me.'

'If we're going to be involved I want to know what's going on.'

'Just tell McKay that I can use him. Hand over the cash and you won't hear any more.'

'How long will it take?'

'Three to four weeks.'

'What do you want, pounds or dollars?'

'Doesn't matter. Whatever's easier.'

'I'll send you the cash tomorrow morning. But I'll want a receipt and I'll want an accounting when it's all over.'

I tried not to smile as I thought of the accounting.

'That's OK, Joe. Send it to me at the office.'

It had taken Hamish McKay just over two days but I'm sure it wasn't longer than necessary or because he enjoyed it. I enjoyed it, but I was more or less an observer.

I saw the ad in *Advertisers' Weekly* the following Friday. It was in the classified section. Brief and innocent.

Moroccan tours company seeks small/medium-sized advertising agency to handle small account £20/30,000 pounds. Box No 742 Advertisers' Weekly. Mercury House London SW2.

I spent two days organising things in Tangier the next weekend. We had had twenty-three responses to the ad, and I sent a cable to Barnes Advertising confirming that they had the account, and asking them to phone their acceptance. They phoned the same evening and I did my Marseilles accent, read them out the copy and told them to put four-inch doubles in *Church*

Times, *The Catholic Herald* and the *Jewish Chronicle*. I don't believe in either favouritism or prejudice.

I got Hacker to give me a list of twenty-five names and addresses and told him what I wanted done by the Post Office Special Unit.

It took two weeks before there was enough material and I phoned Hacker for another meeting. I said it had to be in private and opted for my office.

He sat the other side of my desk opening the envelopes one by one. It took him quite a time and then he looked across at me.

'D'you mean to say Hamish McKay did these.'

'Under my direction he did.'

'Not in the studio at Broadway surely.'

'No, we hired one.'

'And the girls?'

'We hired them, too.'

'I don't want that on the account sheet.'

'We just put it down as models.'

'Not bloody likely we don't.'

'OK, we just bump up the hire-charge for the studio.'

'I don't want to know, mate. It's all yours. What happens next?'

'Just leave it to me. I'll contact you. But I want a telephone number manned round the clock.'

'That's no problem.'

'When it rings they say Post Office Legal Department. They'll ask for Mr Harris. That's me. I'm not there but I'm expected back. Take their number and I'll call them back. Let me know as soon as they call. Here or at home. Answer no questions. Absolutely nothing. OK?'

'OK,' he said reluctantly.

'D'you want a drink?'

'A whisky if you've got one.'

I went into the outer office and got the glasses and the bottle. We were there about another hour. After he had gone I piled up the envelopes and sorted the sheep from the goats. The goats were the ones on my list of names and addresses from Hacker. It took me over an hour because there were two empty envelopes. I went over my desk, the carpet, then the whole of my office but the envelopes stayed empty.

I spent two hours the next morning at the Chambers of one of SIS's barrister advisers. He was obviously mystified by my interest in that particular section of the law but he ploughed through it as I made notes.

I pressed the brass bell at the side of the bright blue door and it buzzed and opened. In the small foyer was an old dear at a desk with a small switchboard. I asked for Mr Pattakos.

'He's not here, I'm afraid.'

'Is Mr Parker in?'

'Yes, but he's very busy.'

'I'd like to see him.'

'What name shall I say?'

'Harris. Mr Harris.'

She mumbled into the telephone and then hung up.

'If you'll take a seat he'll see you in a few minutes. He only sees space reps by appointment you know.'

Parker came down about ten minutes later. He was in his late fifties. White hair, he could have been used by Central Casting for any 'English gentleman' part. He could have played Andy Hardy's father without a touch of make-up.

'Mr Hollis is it?' he said.

'Harris. James Harris.'

'I haven't got more than a couple of minutes I'm afraid.'

'Could I see you in private?'

He looked surprised. 'Is that necessary?'

'I think it would be better.'

When he hesitated I said very softly, 'I've got a warrant for your arrest.'

I followed him slowly up the narrow stairs and into a pleasant modern office. He waved limply towards one of the chairs round the table and sat down himself. He looked tense but not scared as he pushed a couple of files to one side.

'Now,' he said, 'I suppose this is some sort of mistake.'

'You're George Hamilton Parker, a director of the Barnes Advertising Agency Limited, yes?'

'Yes.'

'And you placed advertising on behalf of Moroccan Enterprises?'

'Yes. They're a comparatively new client.'

'You looked into their background of course?'

He frowned. 'No. They paid in advance and there's no way we could check on them, they're based in Morocco.'

'You didn't check with our embassy or the Board of Trade?'

'No.'

'Did you check on their product?'

'There isn't a product. They offer a week's holiday in Tangier.'

'You checked the airline and the accommodation?'

'No. The airline's British charter and we assumed the accommodation's all right.'

'D'you remember the copy in the ad?'

'No.'

I pulled out the ad and put it on the table and pointed to the coupon.

'It says "Send for full details of the good-time you'll get with Moroccan Enterprises".'

He nodded and looked at me, his eyebrows raised.

'Did you produce their reply?'

'No. They said they had brochures already and that

it was better for enquirers to get the material direct from Tangier. People like a foreign post-mark and a stamp.'

'You mean you didn't even see what they were sending through the post?'

'No.'

'I can't believe that, Mr Parker.'

'I assure you it's true.'

I put the brief-case on the table and took out a bundle of the envelopes and pushed them across the table towards him.

'Have a look at those.'

His hands trembled as he picked up the first envelope and slid out the contents. There was the postcard and the original coupon from the ad.

He stared at the postcard then reached for another envelope and went through the same routine.

'They're all the same type of material, Mr Parker. Turn one over and read what's on the back.' I saw his lips moving as he read the words. I knew them by heart because I'd written them. They weren't the best copy I'd ever written but they did the job. On the back of each postcard it said, 'This is just part of the fun you get on a Moroccan Enterprise holiday in Tangier – sin city of North Africa.'

He'd had time to read *War and Peace* before he put the card down and looked across at me.

'There's obviously been a terrible mistake. I'll have to look into it.'

'I'm afraid it's too late for that, Mr Parker. We have already looked into it. You've not only been grossly negligent but you've committed a whole heap of offences.'

'But we had no idea . . .'

'You'll be able to explain that to the court. Meantime I've got warrants to serve on the four directors. Are they all here?'

'I'm afraid that Mr Makins is out.'

'Are the other two here?'

'Only Mr Pattakos.'

'Perhaps you could ask him to step down here and have a word with me.'

'I'll see if I can find him.'

'I'll come with you,' I said.

We went up two floors and the old boy knocked on the door marked *Private* and a voice with an accent called out, 'Come in.'

It was a large room that had probably once been an attic but it was now an office, living quarters and bedroom combined. It smelt faintly aromatic or perhaps it was incense.

The young man sipping coffee in an armchair was good looking but not handsome. More Greek than Cypriot with a light olive skin and soft spaniel eyes. There was nothing of the brigand about him. He sat with his coffee cup poised in front of his mouth as Parker introduced me. When he came to the bit about warrants for arrest Pattakos slowly put down his cup and saucer on the coffee table. The brown eyes looked up at me and he said softly, 'May I see the warrant and your identity card?'

I put both on the table. He glanced at my I.D. but read the warrant carefully. He reached for the telephone without looking and dragged it in front of him. He dialled a number and waited, and lit a cigarette before he spoke.

'*Pyos, ine eki? . . . moo thinete ton Kirio Papadopolos, parakalo . . .*'

The conversation went on for six or seven minutes and he looked at me intently while he was talking. When he hung up he said, 'My lawyer says that all you can do is confiscate the material.'

'That only applies to the charge under the Customs Consolidation Act 1876. The main charges, as you can see, are under the Post Office Act 1953, section eleven.'

'We were deceived for some reason.'

'You were negligent not to check what your clients were doing.'

'The Act specifies "for gain", we made no gain.'

'The Act states the gain may accrue indirectly. Your gain was commission from the journals for placing the ads.'

He gave me a long searching look. 'Can I see the material?'

I gave him half a dozen envelopes and he looked at them and their contents slowly and carefully. Eventually he looked at Parker and said, 'Leave it to me, George. I'll see you later.'

When Parker had left Pattakos leaned back in his chair and lit another cigarette. He closed his eyes as he inhaled and when he opened them he leaned forward towards me.

'You'd better go down the list.'

'What list?'

'The penalties you've got in mind.'

'You've seen the charges.'

'I'm talking about the penalties.'

'It's up to three years' imprisonment for each of you plus fines.'

'And we lose our agency recognition and have to close down.'

'I should think so.'

He nodded slowly. 'My lawyer advises me that there is a defence of "no reasonable cause to suspect" what was going on.'

'That would probably work for an individual but not for a company. Negligence isn't a defence.'

He loosened his tie and lit another cigarette. His brown eyes were neither angry nor disturbed.

'What is it you're after?'

'I'm just serving the warrants.'

He tapped the ash from his cigarette into the ashtray,

still looking at me. 'I'd go up to twenty thousand in sterling or dollars, your choice.'

'You're just getting in deeper, Mr Pattakos. The penalties for bribery are just as heavy.'

'What is it you want?'

'I don't want anything and I advise . . .'

'What do your people want?'

'You mean the Director of Public Prosecutions?'

He shook his head. 'No. I mean that I know we've been framed and I want to know what it's going to cost.'

'What have you got in mind?'

He stared at me for a few moments. 'I'm a politician, not a crook. I'll do whatever is necessary. I don't give a damn about going to prison, that would get me more votes in the next elections than I could hope for now. But it wastes my time, and the organisation needs me right now.'

'So?'

'I could close down the agency.'

'Do the two old boys know what you were up to?'

'No. Of course not.'

'Would you pay them pensions or compensation?'

'No. They were paid a fair price for the agency.'

'I'd better mention that your bank accounts have been frozen.'

'Since when?'

'Since nine o'clock this morning. We've found six but we'll freeze any others we find. Personal as well as business.'

For the first time the brown eyes looked angry. He opened his mouth to speak but lit another cigarette instead.

'OK,' he said. 'What do you want?'

'You close the agency. You don't try and sell it. You give the two old boys a lump sum each of ten thousand. And that's the end of it.'

'What do we get?'

'You don't go to jail. You don't pay fines. You and your partner leave the country within fourteen days. You don't try playing games through the Greek Embassy to stay.'

'How long have I got to decide?'

'A couple of minutes.'

He stubbed out an almost whole cigarette and lit another. As he put down the lighter he said, 'OK. It's a deal.'

I stayed around until he'd put his part in train and then headed for Hacker's office.

His girl said he'd be back by four so I waited. And for some unknown reason I thought of the missing post-cards. At Matlock they'd said, if you've only got two minutes in an office always go for the bottom right-hand drawer.

And there they were, under a copy of *The Spectator*, both of them face down. I turned them face up and I suddenly understood why Hacker didn't get on with girls. They were both of the young blonde who called herself Michelle and was more likely a Maisie from Birmingham. She was about twenty and very pretty. They were the only two shots we had taken of that particular type and I'd had to phone one of SIS's tame psychiatrists to find out what they did. She was well-built and the ropes cut into her firm young breasts and across her belly and her thighs. That was the least abnormal part of the pose and for the rest you'd have to dislike girls an awful lot to get any kind of kick out of doing it or seeing it.

I closed the drawer and left a note on Hacker's desk.

The small agency went out of business ten days later and in about 1960 I saw a picture of Pattakos in *The Times*. He was standing a couple of places from Arch-bishop Makarios who was waving to his fans from a balcony in Athens.

Simon Brett

BIG BOY, LITTLE BOY

Under normal circumstances he would have thrown away the letter as soon as he recognised the cramped handwriting, but Larry Renshaw was in the process of murdering his wife, and needed to focus his mind on something else. So he read it.

Mario, the barman, had handed it over. Having a variety of postal addresses in pubs and bars all over London was a habit Larry had developed in less opulent days, and one that he had not attempted to break after his marriage to Lydia. The sort of letters he received had changed, though; there were fewer instructions from 'business associates', fewer guilty wads of notes buying other people's extramarital secrets; their place had been taken by confirmations of his own sexual assignations, correspondence that could, by the widest distension of the category, be classed as love letters. Marriage had not meant an end of secrets.

But it had meant an upgrading of some of the 'postes restantes'. Gaston's Bar in Albemarle Street was a definite advance on the Stag's Head in Kilburn. And the Savile Row suit, from which he flicked the salt shed by Mario's peanuts, was more elegant than a hotel porter's uniform. The gold identity bracelet that clinked reassuringly on his wrist was more comfortable than a handcuff. And, Larry Renshaw sincerely believed, much more his natural style.

Which was why he had to ensure that he continued to live in that style. He was nearly fifty; he resented the injustices of a world which had kept him so long from his natural milieu; and now that he had finally arrived there, he had no intentions of leaving.

Nor was he going to limit his life-style by removing those elements (other women) of which Lydia disapproved.

Which was why, while he sipped Campari and vodka in Gaston's Bar, he was murdering his wife.

And why he read Peter Mostyn's letter to take his mind off what he was doing.

. . . and those feelings for you haven't changed. I know over thirty years have passed, but those nights we spent together are still the memories I most treasure. I have never had any other friends. *Nothing that has happened and no one I have met since has meant as much to me as the pleasure I got, not only from being with you, but also from being known as* yours, *from being teased at school as your Little Boy.*

I know it didn't mean as much to you, but I flatter myself that you felt something *for me at the time. I remember how once we changed pyjamas, you let me sleep in yours in* your *bed all night. I've never felt closer to you than I did that night, as if I didn't just take on your clothes, but also a bit of you, as if I became you for a little while. I had never felt so happy. Because, though we always looked a little alike, though we were the same height, had the same colouring, I never had your strength of character. Just then, for a moment, I knew what it was like to be Larry Renshaw.*

It was wonderful for me to see you last week. I'm only sorry it was for such a short time. Remember, if there's ever anything *I can do for you, you have only to ask. If you want to meet up again, do ring. I'm only over here sorting out some sort of problem on my uncle's will and, as I'm pretty hard up, I spend most my time in my room at the hotel. But, if I am* out *when you ring, they'll take a message. I'll be going back to France at the end of the week, but I'd really like to see you*

*before then. I sometimes think I'll take my courage in both
hands and come round to your flat, but I know you wouldn't
really like it, particularly now you are* married to that
woman. *It was quite a shock when you told me about your
marriage. I had always had a secret hope that the reason you
never* had *married was . . .'*

Larry stopped reading. Not only had the mention of
his marriage brought his mind back to the murder of
Lydia, he also found the letter distasteful.

It wasn't being the object of a homosexual passion
that worried or challenged him. He had no doubt where
his own tastes lay. He didn't even think he had gone
through a homosexual phase in adolescence, but he had
always had a strong libido, and what other outlet was
there in a boys' boarding school? All the other Big Boys
had had Little Boys, so he had played the games tradition demanded. But, as soon as he had been released
from that particular prison, he had quickly discovered,
and concentrated on, the instinctive pleasures of
heterosexuality.

But Peter Mostyn hadn't changed. He'd make contact every few years, suggesting a lunch, and Larry,
aware that a free meal was one he didn't have to pay for,
would agree to meet. Their conversation would be
stilted, spiralling round topics long dead, and Larry
would finish up his brandy and leave as soon as the bill
arrived. Then, within a week, one of the 'poste
restante' barmen would hand over a letter full of
closely written obsequious gratitude and assurances of
continuing devotion.

Obviously, for Mostyn the dormitory grappling had
meant more, and he had frozen like an insect in the
amber of adolescence. That was what depressed Larry.
He hated the past, he didn't like to think about it. For
him there was always the hope of the big win just
around the next corner, and he would rather concen-
trate on that than on the disasters behind him.

He could forget the past so easily, instinctively sloughing off the skin of one shady failure to slither out with a shining new identity ready for the next infallible scheme. This protean ability had enabled him to melt from stockbroker's clerk to army recruit (after a few bounced cheques); from army reject to mail order manager (after a few missing boxes of ammunition); from mail order manager to pimp (after a few prepaid but undelivered orders); and from pimp to hotel porter (after a police raid). And it had facilitated the latest metamorphosis, from hotel porter to Savile-Row-suited husband of rich neurotic dipsomaniac (just before the inevitable theft inquiry). For Larry change and hope went hand in hand.

So Peter Mostyn's devotion was an unpleasant intrusion. It suggested that, whatever his current identity, there remained in Larry an unchanging core that could still be loved. It threatened his independence in a way the love of women never had. His heterosexual affairs were all brisk and physical, soon ended, leaving in him no adverse emotion that couldn't be erased by another conquest and, in the women, undiluted resentment.

But Peter Mostyn's avowed love was something else, a disagreeable reminder of his continuing identity, almost a *memento mori*. And Peter Mostyn himself was even more of a *memento mori*.

They had met the previous week, for the first time in six years. Once again old habits had died hard, and Larry had instinctively taken the bait of a free meal, in spite of his new opulence.

As soon as he saw Peter Mostyn, he knew it was a bad idea. He felt like Dorian Gray meeting his picture face to face. The Little Boy had aged so unattractively that his appearance was a challenge to Larry's vigour and smartness. After all, they were about the same age – no, hell, Mostyn was younger. At school he had been the

Little Boy to Larry's Big Boy. A couple of forms behind, so a couple of years younger.

And yet to see him, you'd think he was on the verge of death. He had been ill, apparently; Larry seemed to remember his saying something over the lunch about having been ill. Perhaps that explained the long tubular crutches and the general air of debility. But it was no excuse for the teeth and the hair; the improvement of those was quite within his power. OK, most of us lose some teeth, but that doesn't mean we have to go around with a mouth like a drawstring purse. Larry prided himself on his own false teeth. One of the first things he'd done after marrying Lydia had been to set up a series of private dental appointments and have his mouth filled with the best replacements money could buy.

And the hair . . . Larry was thinning a bit and would have been greying but for the discreet preparation he bought from his Jermyn Street hairdresser. But he liked to think that, even if he had been so unfortunate as to lose all his hair, he wouldn't have resorted to a toupee like a small brown mammal that had been run over by a day's traffic on the M1.

And yet that was how Peter Mostyn had appeared, a hobbling creature with concave lips and hair that lacked any credibility. And, to match his physical state, he had demonstrated his emotional crippledom with the same adolescent infatuation and unwholesome self-pity, the same constant assertions that he would do anything for his friend, that he felt his own life to be without value and only likely to take on meaning if it could be used in the service of Larry Renshaw.

Larry didn't like any of it. Particularly he didn't like the constant use of the past tense, as if life from now on would be an increasingly crepuscular experience. He thought in the future tense, and of a future that was infinite, now that he had Lydia's money.

Now that he had Lydia's money . . . He looked at his watch. A quarter to eight. She should be a good five hours dead. Time to put thoughts of that tired old queen Mostyn behind him, and get on with the main business of the day. Time for the dutiful husband to go home and discover his wife's body. Or, if he was really lucky, discover that his sister-in-law had just discovered his wife's body.

He said goodbye loudly to Mario, and made some quip about the barman's new apron. He also asked if the bar-room clock was right and checked his watch against it.

After a lifetime of obscuring details of timing and squeezing alibis from forgotten minutes, it was an amusing novelty to draw attention to time. And to himself.

For the same reason he exchanged memorable banter with the driver of the taxi he picked up in a still light Piccadilly, before settling back for the journey to Abbey Road.

Now he felt supremely confident. He was following his infallible instinct. The plan was the work of a mastermind. He even had a twinge of regret to think that, when he had all Lydia's money, that mind would be lost to crime. But no, he did not intend to hazard his new-found fortune by doing anything mildly risky. He needed freedom to cram into his remaining rich life what he had missed out on in poorer days.

Which was why the murder plan was so good; it contained no risk at all.

In fact, although he did not consciously realise it at the time, he had got the murder plan at the same time that he had got Lydia. She had come ready-packed with her own self-destruct mechanism. The complete kit.

Lydia had fallen in love with Larry when he saved her life, and had married him out of gratitude.

It had happened two years previously. Larry Renshaw had been at the lowest ebb of a career that had known many freak tides. He had been working as a porter at a Park Lane hotel, whose management was beginning to suspect him of helping himself from the wallets, handbags and jewel-cases of the guests. One afternoon he had received a tip-off that they were on to him, and determined to make one last, reasonable-sized haul before another sudden exit and change of identity.

Observation and staff gossip led him to use his pass-key on the door of a Mrs Lydia Phythian, a lady whose Christmas tree appearances in the bar left no doubts about her possession of a considerable stock of jewellery, and whose consumption of gin in the same bar suggested that she might be a little careless in locking away her decorations.

So it proved. Necklaces, brooches, bracelets and rings lay among the pill bottles on the dressing table as casually as stranded seaweed. But there was also in the room something that promised a far richer and less risky haul than a fence's grudging prices for the gems.

There was Mrs Lydia Phythian, in the process of committing suicide.

The scene was classic to the point of being corny. An empty gin bottle clutched in the hand of the snoring figure on the bed. On the bedside table, an empty pill-bottle, dramatically on its side, and, propped against the lamp, a folded sheet of crisp blue monogrammed notepaper.

The first thing Larry did was to read the note.

THIS WAS THE ONLY WAY OUT. NOBODY CARES WHETHER I LIVE OR DIE AND I DON'T WANT TO GO ON JUST BEING A BURDEN. I'VE TRIED, BUT LIFE'S TOO MUCH.

It was undated. Instinctively, Larry put it in his pocket before turning his attention to the figure on the bed. She was deeply asleep, but her pulses were still strong. Remembering some movie with this scene in it, he slapped her face.

Her eyes came woozily open. 'I want to die. Why shouldn't I die?'

'Because there's so much to live for,' he replied, possibly remembering dialogue from the same movie.

Her eyes rolled shut again. He rang for an ambulance. Instinct told him to get an outside line and ring the Emergency Services direct; he didn't want the Manager muscling in on his act.

Then, again following the pattern of the movie, he walked her sagging body up and down, keeping her semi-conscious until help arrived.

Thereafter he just followed instinct. Instinct told him to accompany her in the ambulance to the hospital; instinct told him to return (out of his hotel uniform) to be there when she came round after the ministrations of the stomach pump; instinct told him to continue his visits when she was moved to the recuperative luxury of the Avenue Clinic. And instinct provided the words which assured her that there really was a lot to live for, and that it was insane for a woman as attractive as her to feel unloved, and that he at least appreciated her true worth.

So their marriage three months after she came out of the clinic was really a triumph of instinct.

A couple of days before the registry office ceremony, Larry Renshaw had fixed to see her doctor. 'I felt, you know, that I should know her medical history, now that we're going to be together for life,' he said in a responsible voice. 'I mean, I'm not asking you to give away any professional secrets, but obviously I want to ensure that there isn't a recurrence of the appalling incident which brought us together.'

'Of course.' The doctor was bald, thin and frankly sceptical. He did not seem to be taken in by Larry's performance as the concerned husband-to-be. 'Well, she's a very neurotic woman, she likes to draw attention to herself . . . nothing's going to change her basic character.'

'I thought, being married . . .'

'She's been married a few times before, you must know that.'

'Yes, of course, but she seems to have had pretty bad luck and been landed with a lot of bastards. I thought, given someone who really loves her for herself . . .'

'Oh yes, I'm sure she'd be a lot more stable, given *that*.' The scepticism was now so overt as to be insulting, but Larry didn't risk righteous anger, as the doctor went on, 'The trouble is, Mr Renshaw, women as rich as Mrs Phythian tend to meet up with rather a lot of bastards.'

Larry ignored the second insult. 'What I really wanted to know was—'

'What you really wanted to know,' the doctor interrupted, 'was whether she was likely to attempt suicide again.'

Larry nodded gravely.

'Well, I can't tell you. Someone who takes as many pills and drinks as much as she does is rarely fully rational. This wasn't her first attempt, though it was different from the others.'

'How?'

'The previous ones were more obviously just demands for attention, she made pretty sure that she would be found before anything too serious happened. In this case . . . well, if you hadn't walked into the room, I think she'd have gone the distance. Incidentally . . .'

But Larry spoke before the inevitable question about why he came to be in her room. 'Were there any other differences this time?'

'Small ones. The way she crushed up all the pills into

the gin before she started suggested a more positive approach. And the fact that there was no note . . .'

Larry didn't respond to the quizzical look. When he left, the doctor shook him by the hand and said, with undisguised irony, 'I wouldn't worry. I'm sure everything will work out *for you*.'

The insolent distrust was back in that final emphasis, but mixed in the doctor's voice with another feeling, one of relief. At least a new husband would keep Mrs Phythian out of his surgery for a little while. Just a series of repeat prescriptions for tranquillisers and sleeping pills. And he could still charge her for those.

Subconsciously, Larry knew that the doctor had confirmed how easy it would be for him to murder his wife, but he did not let himself think about it. After all, why should it be necessary?

At first it wasn't. Mrs Lydia Phythian changed her name again (she was almost rivalling her husband in the number of identities she had taken on), and became Mrs Lydia Renshaw. At first the marriage worked pretty well. She enjoyed kitting out her new husband, and he enjoyed being taken round to expensive shops and being treated by her. He found her a surprisingly avid sexual partner and, although he couldn't have subsisted on that diet alone, secret snacks with other women kept him agreeably nourished, and he began to think marriage suited him.

Certainly it brought him a life-style that he had never before experienced. Having been brought up by parents whose middle-class insistence on putting him through minor public school had dragged their living standards down to working-class and below, and then having never been securely wealthy for more than a fortnight, he was well placed to appreciate the large flat in Abbey Road, the country house in Uckfield and the choice of driving a Bentley or a little Mercedes.

In fact, there were only two things about his wife that annoyed him – first, her unwillingness to let him see other women and, second, the restricted amount of pocket money she allowed him.

He had found ways around the second problem; in fact he had reverted to his old ways in order to get round it. He had started, very early in their marriage, stealing from his wife.

At first he had done it indirectly. She had trustingly put him in charge of her portfolio of investments, which made it very easy for him to cream off what he required for his day to day needs. However, a stormy meeting with Lydia's broker and accountant, who threatened to disclose all to their employer, persuaded him to relinquish these responsibilities.

So he started robbing his wife directly. The alcoholic haze in which she habitually moved made this fairly easy. Mislaying a ring or a small necklace, or even finding her notecase empty within a few hours of going to the bank, were common occurrences, and not ones to which she liked to draw attention, since they raised the question of how much her drinking affected her memory.

Larry spent a certain amount of this loot on other women, but the bulk of it he consigned to a suitcase, which every three or four weeks was moved discreetly to another Left Luggage office (premarital habits again dying hard). Over some twenty months of marriage, he had accumulated between twelve and thirteen thousand pounds, which was a comforting hedge against adversity.

But he did not expect adversity. Or at least he did not expect adversity until he discovered that his wife had put a private detective on to him and had compiled a dossier of a fortnight's infidelities.

It was then that he knew he had to murder her, and had to do it quickly, before the meeting with her solicitor which she had mentioned when confronting him with the detective's report. Larry Renshaw had no intention of being divorced from his wife's money.

As soon as he had made the decision, the murder plan that he had shut up in the Left Luggage locker of his subconscious was revealed by a simple turn of a key. It was so simple, he glowed from the beauty of it.

He went through it again as he sat in the cab on the way to Abbey Road. The timing was perfect; there was no way it could fail.

Every three months Lydia spent four days at a health farm. The aim was not primarily to dry her out, but to put a temporary brake on the runaway deterioration of her physical charms. However, the strictness of the fashionable institution chosen to take on this hopeless task meant that the visit did have the side-effect of keeping her off alcohol for its duration. The natural consequence of this was that on the afternoon of her return she would, regular as clockwork, irrigate her parched system with at least half a bottle of gin.

And that was all the plan needed. His instinct told him it could not fail.

He had made the preparations that morning, almost joyously. He had whistled softly as he worked. There was so little to do. Crush up the pills into the gin bottle, place the suicide note in the desk drawer and set out to spend his day in company. No part of that day was to be unaccounted for. Gaston's Bar was only the last link in a long chain of alibi.

During the day, he had probed at the plan, testing it for weaknesses, and found none.

Suppose Lydia thought the gin tasted funny . . . ? She wouldn't, in her haste. Anyway, in her descriptions of the previous attempt, she had said there was no taste. It had been, she said, just like drinking it neat, and getting gently drowsier and drowsier. A quiet end. Not an unattractive one.

Suppose the police found out about the private detective and the appointment with the solicitor ... ? Wouldn't they begin to suspect the dead woman's husband ... ? No, if anything that strengthened his case. Disillusioned by yet another man, depressed by the prospect of yet another divorce, she had taken the quickest way out. True, it didn't put her husband in a very good light, but Larry was not worried about that. So long as he inherited, he didn't care what people thought.

Suppose she had already made a will which disinherited him ... ? But no, he knew she hadn't. That was what she had set up with the solicitor for the next day. And Larry had been present when she made her previous will that named him, her husband, as sole legatee.

No, his instinct told him nothing could go wrong.

He paid off the taxi-driver, and told him an Irish joke he had heard in the course of the day. He then went into their block of flats, told the porter the same Irish joke, and asked if he could check the right time. Eight-seventeen. Never had there been a better-documented day.

As he went up in the lift, he wondered if the final refinement to the plan had happened. It wasn't essential, but it would have been nice. Lydia's sister had said she would drop round for the evening. If she could actually have discovered the body ... Still, she was notoriously bad about time and you can't have everything. But it would be nice ...

Everything played into his hands. On the landing he met a neighbour just about to walk his chihuahua. Larry greeted them cheerfully and checked the time. His confidence was huge. He enjoyed being a criminal mastermind.

36

For the benefit of the departing neighbour and because he was going to play the part to the hilt, he called
out cheerily, 'Good evening, darling!' as he unlocked
the front door.

'Good evening, *darling*,' said Lydia.

As soon as he saw her, he knew that she knew everything. She sat poised on the sofa and on the glass coffee
table in front of her were the bottle of gin and the suicide
note. If they had been labelled in a courtroom, they
couldn't have been more clearly marked as evidence.
On a table to the side of the sofa stood a half-empty
bottle of gin. The bloody, boozy bitch – she couldn't
even wait until she got home, she'd taken on new
supplies on the way back from the health farm.

'Well, Larry, I dare say you're surprised to see me.'

'A little,' he said easily, and smiled what he had
always believed to be a charming smile.

'I think I'll have quite a lot to say to my solicitor
tomorrow.'

He laughed lightly.

'After I've been to the police,' she continued.

His next laugh was more brittle.

'Yes, Larry, there are quite a few things to talk about.
For a start, I've just done an inventory of my jewellery.
And do you know, I think I've suddenly realised why
you appeared in my hotel room that fateful afternoon.
Once a thief, always a thief. But murder . . . that's
going up a league for you, isn't it?'

The gin hadn't got to her; she was speaking with cold
coherence. Larry slowed down his mind to match her
logical deliberation. He walked over to his desk in the
corner by the door. When he turned round, he was
holding the gun he kept in its drawer.

Lydia laughed, loudly and unattractively, as if in
derision of his manhood. 'Oh, come on, Larry, that's
not very subtle. No, your other little scheme was quite

clever, I'll give you that. But to shoot me . . . They'd never let you inherit. You aren't allowed to profit from a crime.'

'I'm not going to shoot you.' He moved across and pointed the gun at her head. 'I'm going to make you drink from that other gin bottle.'

Again he got the harsh, challenging laugh. 'Oh, come on, sweetie. What kind of threat is that? There's a basic fault in your logic. You can't make people kill themselves by threatening to kill them. If you gotta go, who cares about the method? And if you intend to kill me, I'll ensure that you do it the way that gives you most trouble. Shoot away, sweetie.'

Involuntarily, he lowered the arm holding the gun.

She laughed again.

'Anyway, I'm bored with this.' She rose from the sofa. 'I'm going to ring the police. I've had enough of being married to a criminal mastermind.'

The taunt so exactly reflected his self-image that it stung like a blow. His gun-arm stiffened again, and he shot his wife in the temple, as she made her way towards the telephone.

There was a lot of blood. At first he stood there mesmerised by how much blood there was, but then, as the flow stopped, his mind started to work again.

Its deliberations were not comforting. He had blown it. The best he could hope for now was escape.

Unnaturally calm, he went to the telephone. He rang Heathrow. There was a ten o'clock flight. Yes, there was a seat. He booked it.

He took the spare cash from Lydia's handbag. Under ten pounds. She hadn't been to the bank since her return from the health farm. Still, he could use a credit card to pay for the ticket.

He went into the bedroom, where her jewellery lay in its customary disarray. He reached out for a diamond choker.

But no. Suppose the Customs searched him? That was just the sort of trouble he had to avoid. For the same reason he couldn't take the jewellery from his case in the Left Luggage office. Where was it now, anyway? Oh no, Liverpool Street. Fumes of panic rose to his brain. There wouldn't be time. Or would there? Maybe if he just got the money from the case and—

The doorbell rang.

Oh my God! Lydia's sister!

He grabbed a suitcase, threw in his pyjamas and a clean shirt, then rushed into the kitchen, opened the back door and ran down the fire escape.

Peter Mostyn's cottage was in the Department of Lot. The nearest large town was Cahors, the nearest small town was Montaigu-de-Quercy, but neither was very near. The cottage itself was small and primitive; Mostyn was not a British trendy making a fashionable home in France, he had moved there in search of obscurity and lived very cheaply, constantly calculating how many years he could remain there on the dwindling capital he had been left by a remote uncle, and hoping that it would last out his lifetime. He didn't have more contact with the locals than weekly shopping demanded, and both sides seemed happy with this arrangement.

Larry Renshaw arrived there on the third night after Lydia's death. He had travelled unobtrusively by local trains, thumbed lifts and long stretches of cross-country walking, sleeping in the fields by night. He had sold his Savile Row suit for a tenth of its value in a Paris second-hand clothes shop, where he had bought a set of stained blue overalls, which made him less conspicuous tramping along the sun-baked roads of France. His passport and gold identity bracelet were secure in an inside pocket.

If there was any chase, he reckoned he was ahead of it.

It had been dark for about four hours when he reached the cottage. It was a warm summer night. The countryside was dry and brittle, needing rain. Although the occasional car had flashed past on the narrow local roads, he had not met any pedestrians.

There was a meagre slice of moon which showed him enough to dash another hope. In the back of his mind had lurked the possibility that Mostyn, in spite of his constant assertions of poverty, lived in luxury and would prove as well-fleshed a body as Lydia to batten on. But the crumbling exterior of the cottage told him that the long-term solution to his problems would have to lie elsewhere. The building had hardly changed at all through many generations of peasant owners.

And when Mostyn came to the door, he could have been the latest representative of that peasant dynasty. His wig was off, he wore a shapeless sort of nightshirt and clutched a candle-holder out of a Dickens television serial. The toothless lips moved uneasily and in his eye was an old peasant distrust of outsiders.

That expression vanished as soon as he recognised his visitor.

'Larry. I hoped you'd come to me. I read about it in the papers. Come inside. You'll be safe here.'

Safe he certainly was. Mostyn's limited social round meant that there was no danger of the newcomer being recognised. No danger of his ever being seen. For three days the only person Larry Renshaw saw was Peter Mostyn.

And Peter Mostyn still hadn't changed at all. He remained a pathetic cripple, rendered even more pathetic by his cringing devotion. For him Renshaw's appearance was the answer to a prayer. Now at last he had the object of his affections in his own home. He was in seventh heaven.

Renshaw wasn't embarrassed by the devotion; he

knew Mostyn was far too diffident to try and force unwelcome attentions on him. For a little while at least he had found sanctuary, and was content for a couple of days to sit and drink his host's brandy and assess his position.

The assessment wasn't encouraging. Everything had turned sour. All the careful plans he had laid for Lydia's death now worked against him. The elaborate fixing of the time of his arrival at the flat no longer established his alibi; it now pointed the finger of murder at him. Even after he'd shot her, he might have been able to sort something out, but for that bloody sister of hers ringing the bell and making him panic. Everything had turned out wrong.

On the third evening, as he sat silent at the table, savagely drinking brandy while Mostyn watched him, Renshaw shouted out against the injustice of it all. 'That bloody bitch!'

'Lydia?' asked Mostyn hesitantly.

'No, you fool. Her sister. If she hadn't turned up just at that moment, I'd have got away with it. I'd have thought of something.'

'At what moment?'

'Just after I'd shot Lydia. She rang the bell.'

'What – about eight-thirty?'

'Yes.'

Mostyn paled beneath his toupee. 'That wasn't Lydia's sister.'

'What? How do you know?'

'It was me.' Renshaw looked at him. 'It was me. I was flying back the next morning. You hadn't *rung*. I so wanted to see you before I left. I came to the flats. I didn't *intend* to go in. But I asked the porter if you were there and he said you'd just arrived . . .'

'It was you! You bloody fool, why didn't you say?'

'I didn't know what had happened. I just—'

'You idiot! You bloody idiot!' The frustration of the

41

last few days and the brandy came together in a wave of fury. Renshaw seized Mostyn by the lapels and shook him. 'If I had known it was you . . . You could have saved my life. You bloody fool! You . . .'

'I didn't know. I didn't know,' the Little Boy whimpered. 'When there was no reply, I just went back to the hotel. Honestly, if I'd known what was happening . . . I'd do anything for you, you *know*. Anything . . .'

Renshaw slackened his grasp on Mostyn's lapels and returned to Mostyn's brandy.

It was the next day that he took up the offer. They sat over the debris of lunch. 'Peter, you said you'd do anything for me . . .'

'Of course, and I meant it. My life hasn't been much, you're the only person that matters to me. I'd do anything for you. I'll look after you here for as long as—'

'I'm not staying here. I have to get away.'

Mostyn's face betrayed his hurt. Renshaw ignored it and continued, 'For that I need money.'

'I've told you, you can have anything that I—'

'No, I know you haven't got any money. Not real money. But I have. In the Left Luggage office at Liverpool Street Station I have over twelve thousand pounds in cash and jewellery.' Renshaw looked at Mostyn with the smile he had always believed to be charming. 'I want you to go to England to fetch it for me.'

'What? But I'd never get it back over here.'

'Yes, you would. You're the ideal smuggler. You put the stuff in your crutches. They'd never suspect someone like you.'

'But I—'

Renshaw looked hurt. 'You said you'd do anything for me . . .'

'Well, I would, but—'

'You can go into Cahors tomorrow and fix the flight.'

'But . . . but that means you'll leave me again.'

'For a little while, yes. I'd come back,' Renshaw lied.

'I . . .'

'Please do it for me, please . . .' Renshaw put on an expression he knew to be vulnerable.

'All right, I will.'

'Bless you, bless you. Come on, let's drink to it.'

'I don't drink much. It makes me sleepy. I haven't got the head for it. I—'

'Come on, drink.'

Mostyn hadn't got the head for it. As the afternoon progressed, he became more and more embarrassingly devoted. Then he fell into a comatose sleep.

The day after next the plane ticket was on the dining-room table, next to Peter Mostyn's passport. Upstairs his small case was packed ready. He was to fly from Paris in three days' time, on the Wednesday. He would be back at the cottage by the weekend. With the money and jewels which would be Renshaw's lifeline.

Renshaw's confidence started to return. With money in his pocket, everything would once more become possible. Twelve thousand pounds was plenty to buy a new identity and start again. Talent like his, he knew, could not be kept down for long.

Mostyn was obviously uneasy about the task ahead of him, but he had been carefully briefed and he'd manage it all right. The Big Boy was entrusting him with a mission and the Little Boy would see that it was efficiently discharged.

A new harmony came into their relationship. Now that his escape had a date on it, Renshaw could relax and even be pleasant to his protector. Mostyn glowed with gratitude for the attention. It did not take much to make him happy, Renshaw thought contemptuously. Once again, as he looked at the prematurely aged and crippled figure, he found it incongruous that their bodies had ever touched. Mostyn had never been other than pathetic.

Still, he was useful. And, though it was making huge inroads into his carefully husbanded wealth, he kept the supply of brandy flowing. Renshaw topped up his tumbler again after lunch on the Monday afternoon.

It was then that there was a knock at the door. Mostyn leapt nervously to the window to check out the visitor. When he looked back at Renshaw, his face had even less colour under its thatch. 'It's a gendarme.'

Moving quickly and efficiently, Larry Renshaw picked up his dirty plate, together with the brandy bottle and tumbler, and went upstairs. His bedroom window was above the sloping roof of the porch. If anyone came up, he would be able to make a quick getaway.

He heard conversation downstairs, but it was too indistinct and his knowledge of French too limited for him to understand it. Then he heard the front door shut. From his window he saw the gendarme go to his bike and cycle off towards Montaigu-de-Quercy.

He gave it five minutes and went downstairs. Peter Mostyn sat at the table, literally shaking.

'What the hell's the matter?'

'The gendarme . . . he asked if I had seen you.'

'So you said you hadn't.'

'Yes, but . . .'

'But what? That's all there is to it, surely. There's been an Interpol alert to check out any contacts I might have abroad. They got your name from my address book back at the flat. So now the local bobby here has done his bit and will report back that you haven't seen me since last week in London. End of story. I'm glad it's happened; at least now I don't have to wait for it.'

'Yes, but, Larry, look at the state I'm in.'

'You'll calm down. Come on. OK, it was a shock, but you'll get over it.'

'That's not what I mean. What I'm saying is, if I'm in this state now, I just won't be able to go through with what I'm supposed to be doing on Wednesday.'

'Look, for Christ's sake, all you have to do is to catch a plane to London, go to the Liverpool Street Left Luggage office, get the case, go to somewhere conveniently quiet, load the stuff into your crutches and come back here. There's no danger.'

'I can't do it, Larry. I *can't*. I'll crack up. I'll give myself away somehow. If I were like you, I could do it. You've always had a strong nerve for that sort of thing. I wish it were you who was going to do it, because I know you *could*. But I just . . .'

He petered out. Anger invaded Renshaw. 'Listen, you little worm, you've got to do it! Good God, you've said enough times you'd do anything for me; and now, the first time I ask for something, you're bloody chicken.'

'Larry, I would do anything for you, I would. But I just don't think I *can* go through with this. I'd mess it up somehow. Honestly, Larry, if there were anything *else* I could do . . .'

'Anything else? How about getting me off the murder charge? Maybe you'd like to do that instead?' Renshaw asked with acid sarcasm.

'If I could . . . Or if I had enough money to be any use . . . Or if—'

'Oh, shut up, you useless little queen!' Larry Renshaw stomped savagely upstairs with the brandy bottle.

They did not speak to each other for over twenty-four hours.

But the next evening, as he lay on the bed drinking brandy, watching the declining sun tinge the scrubby oak trees of the hillside with gold, Renshaw's instinct started to take over again. It was a warm feeling. Once

45

more he felt protected. His instinct was an Almighty Big Boy, looking after him, guiding him, showing him the way forward, as it always had done before.

After about an hour, he heard the front door and saw Mostyn setting off down the road that led to Montaigu-de-Quercy. Again. He'd been out more than once since their row. No doubt going to buy more brandy as a peace offering. Poor little sod. Renshaw chuckled to himself at the aptness of the description.

Alone in the cottage, he dozed. The bang of the door on Mostyn's return woke him. And he was not surprised to wake up with his plan of campaign worked out in every detail.

Peter Mostyn looked up like a mongrel fearing a kick, but Larry Renshaw smiled at him and was amused to see how gratefully the expression changed. Mostyn had all the weakness of the sort of women Renshaw had spent his life avoiding.

'Larry, look, I'm terribly sorry about yesterday afternoon. I was just a coward. Look, I really *do* want to do something for you. You know I'd give my life for you if I thought it'd be any use. It's been a pretty wasted life, I'd like it to do *something* valuable.'

'But not go to London and pick up my things?' Renshaw asked lightly.

'I just don't think I *could*, Larry, I don't think I have it *in me*. But I will go to London tomorrow. There is something else that I can do for you. I *can* help you. I *have* helped you already. I—'

'Never mind.' Renshaw spread his hands in a magnanimous gesture of forgiveness. 'Never mind. Listen, Peter,' he went on intimately, 'I behaved like a swine yesterday and I want to apologise. I'm sorry, this whole thing's been a dreadful strain, and I just haven't been appreciating all you're doing for me. Please forgive me.'

'You've been fine. I . . .' Mostyn's expression

hovered between surprise and delight at his friend's change of behaviour.

'No, I've been being a swine. Peace offering.' He drew his hand out of his pocket and held it towards Mostyn.

'But you don't want to give me that. It's your identity bracelet, it's got your name on. And it's gold. I mean, you'd—'

'Please . . .'

Mostyn took the bracelet and slipped it on to his thin wrist.

'Listen, Peter, I've been so screwed up that I just haven't been thinking straight. Forget the money in London. Maybe I'll get it someday, maybe I won't. The important thing is that I'm safe at the moment, with a *friend*. A very good friend. Peter, what I want to ask is . . . can I stay here for a bit?' He looked up humbly. 'If you don't mind.'

'Mind? Look, you know, Larry, I'd be delighted. *Delighted*. You don't have to ask that.'

'Bless you, Peter.' Renshaw spoke softly, as if choked by emotion. Then he perked up. 'If that's settled then, let's drink on it.'

'I won't, thank you, Larry. You know it only makes me sleepy.'

'Oh, come on, Peter. If we're going to live together, we've got to learn to enjoy the same hobbies.' And he filled two tumblers with brandy.

The prospect opened up by the words 'live together' was too much for Mostyn. There were tears in his eyes as he drained his first drink.

It was about an hour and a half later when Renshaw judged the moment to be right. Mostyn was slurring his words and yawning, but still conscious. His eyes focused in pleasure for a moment when Renshaw murmured, 'Why don't we go upstairs?'

'Whaddya mean?'

'You know what I mean.' He giggled.

'Really? Really?'

Renshaw nodded.

Mostyn rose, swaying, to his feet. 'Where are my crutches?'

'They won't help you stand up straight in the state you're in.' Renshaw giggled again, and Mostyn joined in. Renshaw ruffled his Little Boy's hair, and the toupee came off in his hand.

'Gimme thaback.'

'When I come upstairs,' Renshaw murmured softly. Then, in an even lower whisper, 'Go up to my room, get my pyjamas, put them on and get into my bed. I'll be up soon.'

Mostyn smiled with fuddled pleasure, and started off up the stairs. Renshaw heard the uneven footsteps in his room above, then the hobbling noises of undressing, the thump of a body hitting the bed and soon, predictably, silence.

He sat for about a quarter of an hour finishing his drink. Then, whistling softly, he started to make his preparations.

He moved slowly, but efficiently, following the infallible dictates of his instinct. First he went into the little bathroom and shaved off his remaining hair. It took a surprisingly short time. Then he removed his false teeth and put them in a glass of water.

He went cautiously up the stairs and inched open the door of his bedroom. As expected, Mostyn lay unconscious from the unaccustomed alcohol.

Unhurriedly, Renshaw placed the glass of teeth on the bedside table. Then he changed into the clothes Mostyn had just abandoned on the floor. He went into the other bedroom, picked up the overnight case that had been packed, and returned downstairs.

He picked up the air ticket and passport, which still

lay accusingly on the dining table. He put on the toupee and compared his reflection with the passport photograph. The picture was ten years old and the resemblance quite sufficient. He picked up the crutches and tried them until he could reproduce the limp that appeared in the 'Special Peculiarities' section.

Then he picked up the half-full brandy bottle, another unopened one and the candle on the table, and went upstairs.

The Little Boy lay on his Big Boy's bed, in his Big Boy's pyjamas, even wearing his Big Boy's gold identity bracelet, but was in no state to appreciate this longed-for felicity. He did not stir as his Big Boy sprinkled brandy over the bedclothes, the rush matting and the wooden floor boards. Nor did he stir when his Big Boy laid the lighted candle on the floor and watched its flames spread.

Larry Renshaw felt the usual confidence that following his instinct produced, as he travelled back to London in the identity of Peter Mostyn. He even found that there were compensations in being a pathetic, toothless cripple on crutches. People made way for him at the airport and helped him with his bags.

On the plane he mused comfortably about his next movements. Certainly his first port of call must be the Left Luggage office at Liverpool Street . . . And then probably one of the fences he already knew, to turn the jewellery into cash . . . Then, who could say? Possibly abroad again . . . Certainly a new identity . . .

But there was no hurry. That was the luxury his instinct had achieved for him. In Mostyn's identity he was safe for as long as he could stand being such a pathetic figure. There was no hurry.

He felt tense as he approached Passport Control at Heathrow. Not frightened – he was confident that his instinct would see him through – but tense. After all, if there was a moment when his identity was most likely to be questioned, this was it. But if he was accepted here as Peter Mostyn, then he had nothing more to worry about.

It was slightly unnerving, because the Passport Officer seemed to be expecting him. 'Ah, Mr Mostyn,' he said. 'If you'd just take a seat here for a moment, I'll tell them you've arrived.'

'But I—' No, better not to make a scene. Reserve righteous indignation for later. Must be some minor mix-up. He imagined how feebly Peter Mostyn would whine at the nuisances of bureaucracy.

He didn't have long to wait. Two men in raincoats arrived and asked him to go with them to a small room. They did not speak again until they were all seated.

'Now,' said the man who seemed to be senior, 'let's talk about the murder of Mrs Lydia Renshaw.'

'Mrs Lydia Renshaw?' echoed Larry Renshaw, bemused. 'But I'm Peter Mostyn.'

'Yes,' said the man, 'we know that. There's no question about that. And that's why we want to talk to you about the murder of Mrs Lydia Renshaw.'

'But . . . why?' Larry Renshaw asked, quite as pathetically as Peter Mostyn would have done.

'Why?' The man seemed puzzled. 'Well, because of your letter of confession that arrived this morning.'

It was some time before he actually saw the document that had incriminated him, but it didn't take him long to imagine its contents.

Because of his long-standing homosexual attraction to Larry Renshaw, Peter Mostyn had gone round to see him the evening before he was due to return to his home in France. At the block of flats in Abbey Road (where he was seen by the porter) he had found, not Renshaw, but Renshaw's wife, the woman who, in his eyes, had irrevocably alienated the affections of his friend. An argument had ensued, in the course of which he had shot his rival. Larry Renshaw, returning to his flat, seeing his wife's body and guessing what had happened, had immediately set off for France in pursuit of the murderer. It was Renshaw's arrival at his home that had prompted Peter Mostyn to make a clean breast of what he had done.

This put Larry Renshaw in a rather difficult position. Since he was now innocent, he could in theory claim back his own identity. But he had a nasty feeling that that would raise more questions than it would answer.

His instinct, now diminished to a limping, apologetic, pathetic thing, advised him to remain as Peter Mostyn, the Little Boy who had made the supreme sacrifice to protect his Big Boy.

So it was as Peter Mostyn that he was charged with, and found guilty of, the murder of Mrs Lydia Renshaw.

And it was as Peter Mostyn that he was later charged with, and found guilty of, the murder of Larry Renshaw.

Celia Dale

BLACK MUSEUM

I have never disliked anyone as much as I came to
dislike Reggie Tyrrell. I admit he had magnetism – the
magnetism that comes not only from immense conceit
but from the cleverness that justifies it, to some extent.
Certainly he had no physical charms to be conceited
about – although he was. He was a short, wiry man –
stringy, really, because when I met him first he was in
his forties and the muscle that had made him (so he all
too often told one) a fine athlete at university had
shrunk to sinew. In bathing trunks and burned by the
sun (he lived half the year in a villa in southern Spain,
up in the hills behind Marbella) he looked like a bundle
of leather bootlaces or one of the small, slightly sinister
lizards that darted about his terraces, gulping flies.

One of the flies he gulped was my friend Pamela,
which is how I met him. She and her mother went for a
spring holiday in Marbella and when they came back
Pamela had a sort of muted glow about her. Pamela is a
muted kind of person. We met at school, where she was
a prefect but never Head Girl. Then she was secretary
to some big wheel in a faceless conglomerate and for
years had an affair with one of the directors – a nice
man, I often met him, but of course heavily married and
no intention of getting free. And then he died of a
coronary one day at home and the first Pamela heard of
it was when she came into the office next morning. She

had to hide it all and sweat it out alone – I saw a lot of her then and I hope I helped. But it broke her up and she became even more muted than she'd been before, allowing herself to be dominated by her tiresome mother.

My marriage was on the rocks soon after – no special reason, I just couldn't stand him any more, he was so totally boring – so I didn't see much of her for a while; but we always kept in touch, and when we met soon after her holiday she had, as I said, this sort of muted glow.

'Did you meet anybody?' I asked. I always asked that.

'Well . . .' She has this fair skin that actually blushes sometimes, a nuisance but rather sweet. 'We met Reggie Tyrrell.'

'Who?'

'Reginald Tyrrell. You know, the writer.'

'What, the crime man? That Tyrrell?'

'Yes. He said he'd ring up when he came back to England but I don't expect he will.'

I must admit I was impressed. Everyone knew Reginald Tyrrell, if not from his books then from his journalism, radio and television. He'd made himself the absolute ultimate expert in murder; apart from his own apparently inexhaustible flow of books and articles on crime, not a symposium or a TV discussion or a preface to some book about murder but Reginald Tyrrell's name appeared on it. He had enormous knowledge, not only of well-known cases but of the more obscure; and he was a past-master at squeezing the last drop of blood from a corpse – no matter how well investigated already he'd find some new thing about it, or some new psychological slant. And somehow he always managed to make it sexy; an old lady poisoned for her money in 1892 had undertones of unspeakable sexual nastiness when Reggie wrote about it.

'What's he like?' I asked.

'He's rather sweet.'

Sweet! I ask you!

He did ring her up when he came back to London in May, and by August they were married. He'd been married three times before and was very vain of the fact. I think Pamela deliberately kept me from meeting him until it was practically all sealed and signed – I suppose she knew I wouldn't approve. So I met him first at their engagement party – Claridges, no less, and nothing but champagne, and Pamela in a sort of daze but with a confidence I'd never seen in her before. Masses of people there – minor Jet Set and publishers and film and television people and other authors whose names one knew and several high-ranking policemen and a famous pathologist. It was a really glossy affair.

They were both by the door, receiving. 'So this is Dinah,' he said, keeping my hand. 'Pam's best friend.'

I don't know what I'd expected. One knew his face, of course, from photographs, but I hadn't realised he was so short and so ugly. He was, as I've said, leathery, and only about five foot six. His hair was greying but thick, rather wiry, worn rather too long for a man over thirty; his nose was aggressive, his mouth too broad. He had very big teeth. His eyes were grey, and he used them to peer ardently at me as he still kept my hand, selling me the idea of how good a friend I was to his bride-to-be while at the same time a desirable woman. It was corny as hell.

Later I saw him caressing the buttocks of some nubile young columnist, kissing the hand of a television actress and the cheek of a fashionable public relations lady. Not the way a man should behave at his own engagement party. I avoided saying goodbye to either of them and went home in a rage. Poor silly Pamela!

*

I had to be friends with them both, of course – I even went to the wedding – for I didn't want to drop Pamela after all these years and I was sure she'd be needing a friend before long, married to that self-satisfied shit. But, wonder of wonders, the marriage seemed a success. When we dined together from time to time he was almost cloyingly attentive to her while still managing to beam a wolf gleam or two towards me from those slightly bloodshot eyes. He was an amusing talker, but sooner or later always brought the conversation round to his own subject – himself and his mastery of Criminology. Apart from his theories on the identity of Jack the Ripper or the murderer of Julia Wallace, he loved to embark on details of lesser known and usually squalid mysteries – poor middle-aged prostitutes disembowelled on rubbish tips or drunken farmers poisoned by their moronic wives. More than this, he had a large collection of relics of various crimes of which he was disgustingly proud, acquired God knows how – from lawyers, detectives, pathologists, amongst whom he had a great number of acquaintances. It was his delight to take one on a tour round this beastly little Black Museum after dinner, when he would explain the relevance of that fragment of bloodstained wallpaper or the singular significance of the yellowed upper denture retrieved from some murderer's cabbage patch. It was absolutely revolting.

But of course it was fascinating too. And he knew it – and knew how to exploit that fascination, the urge to life that fear of death promotes, the bizarre beneath the humdrum, the ultimate orgasm of violent death (his phrases, needless to say). After all, everyone likes a good murder; and Reggie's murders were very good, as his pretty house in St John's Wood, his villa in Spain, his three ex-wives, his Bentley and champagne and custom-made shirts proved.

They went off to the villa for the winter, and as I was

rather preoccupied then with a new man (he didn't work out) I lost touch with them for a while. Pamela wrote and seemed happy. Then one day Reggie rang up. He was back in London ahead of Pamela to do a rush television adaptation of a famous trial, and he asked me to do some work for him – checking dates, researching death certificates – as he was short of time and hadn't a secretary. I was at a loose end just then, so I did. And when Pamela came back to London in April I went on working for him – it quite suited me not to be tied to a regular job. And I have to admit, it was rather fascinating.

Pamela looked blooming but she was more reserved. She had always been quiet but whereas it had been because she was uncertain and timid, now it held confidence. When we met for a girls' lunch and gossip she was very much Mrs Reginald Tyrrell; she wouldn't open up at all about him, not what he was actually *like*. All she would say was that he was 'very sweet', very generous; he worked very hard, they had lots of social life, they were very happy.

'Don't you find all those corpses and blood a bit much?' I asked, a bit bitchily, for her *grande-damerie* was beginning to irritate me. She was only Pamela, for God's sake!

She looked away for a moment, then back with a placid smile. 'I don't notice it. It's his work, after all.'

'But the Black Museum? Those bloodstained bits and pieces and all those ghastly photographs? Knowing he's back to dinner all freshly scrubbed from some sneak view of a post-mortem?'

She blushed. 'Don't be silly, Dinah.'

Of course what I really wanted to know was what he was like in bed with her. But I hadn't quite got the nerve to ask her that.

*

I went out to Rojas and stayed with them twice the next winter. I'd done some more research for him and took the results with me. He was easy to work for, very well organised, writing for three hours every morning and another two after tea, when we'd collate my material. The villa was beautiful, up in the hills with a distant view of the sea, with a swimming-pool and a garden dripping with bougainvillea and geraniums in huge pots and a guest wing with its own terrace and little kitchen. They had a fair circle of friends out there, for Reggie was quite a celebrity, especially in an expatriate community. While he basked in it all, stroking the women and rattling off anecdotes of arsenic and old lace, Pamela ran the household quietly, speaking a careful Spanish to the plump, large-eyed local girls who cooked and cleaned, an efficient wife and hostess. It was a pretty good life for my little school chum who had never managed to make it either to prefect or Chairman's wife.

There was a big murder trial at the Old Bailey the following March (three old age pensioners dug up in the garden of a Sunset Home and all for the sake of their pension books) and Reggie came back to London on his own for it, as he always did. Murder trials were for him what performances at La Scala or Covent Garden are to opera buffs – essential in themselves but also for being seen to be there. This time he wanted me not only to sit in on the trial with him as I had before but also to take notes of some disgusting details he ferreted out unofficially for the book he was planning to write, but that I refused. Going to trials, checking dates and death certificates and bequests in wills was one thing, formaldehyde and your actual murder scenes quite another, it turned me up and I wouldn't do it. So he borrowed a typist from the defence lawyer's office and used her – and that is just what I mean.

I couldn't believe it, not at first. I mean, it was so blatant. Even after Pamela came back for the summer Tracy was still everywhere with him, all bangles and bubble-cut, typing away in the study in St John's Wood, trotting about after him to police stations and mortuaries and the houses of the bereaved with her notebook and biro at the ready. He had been used to typing direct himself, but now he spent hours shut up with Tracy dictating his material to her – or so it was assumed. She did go back to her own home at night, but often he drove her. I simply couldn't believe it.

Pamela gave no sign she noticed anything. She ran the house, hostessed his parties, stood as his lady everywhere, as quiet and undemanding as she had always been. She must have known – even she couldn't have been such a fool. Sometimes I caught a rather frosty glint in her eyes as she smiled at Tracy over their working lunch, but otherwise she gave absolutely no sign.

When she and Reggie went back to the villa in October, Tracy returned to her lawyers' office; the affair was apparently over.

'How do you manage without your faithful slave?' I asked maliciously when I stayed with them there before Christmas.

He gave me one of his lizard looks. 'Who d'you mean – Tracy?' I nodded, he shrugged with a yellow-toothed grin. 'Perfectly well. I'm self-sufficient, you know.'

'Pamela must miss having her underfoot.'

'Me?' Pamela smiled coolly. 'It makes no difference to me. I really didn't notice her.'

Because of Tracy I began to keep a closer eye on Reggie, both on his solo returns to London as well as when I stayed with them at Rojas. In London I hadn't much chance; he came back for only a few days to attend yet another murder trial and this time he didn't suggest I went with him. Apart from dinner one evening, after which he insisted on showing me a new series of pictures of grisly forensic processes which, with great glee, he had managed to acquire from one of his slightly bent police contacts, he went his own way and was soon back at the villa. I think he realised that I now really mistrusted him, and although this seemed to amuse him and feed his vanity, he dropped me.

But I still did research for him – I could suit myself when I did it and the work itself had come to have a kind of fascination. I took the results out to him at Rojas on my first visit that winter and saw, with rising anger and dismay, that he was in pursuit of a monolithic Swedish girl, wife of one of the large foreign colony there, a blonde Valkyrie always half naked and a good head taller than he was. Again, Pamela seemed to notice nothing and treated Ingrid or whatever her name was with the same mild friendliness as everyone else at the vacuous social gatherings that made up life there. How she could have so little pride . . . !

When I went back the second time, in March, Ingrid and her husband had gone. The expatriate colony had shrunk a little, life was rather dull and Reggie was working. He had his own rooms at the end of the villa – bedroom, bathroom and study – and often wouldn't appear till drinks time at sundown. During the day Pamela and I lazed, swam in the pool, drove into the hills or along to Malaga. We didn't talk much; she had always been quiet and now the quiet had become a sort of withdrawal, at least from me – she simply did not seem to want to talk about anything much. And I couldn't really bring myself to say anything to her that touched on Reggie.

The weather was wonderful – mild and blue and the grass on the hillsides still green and thick with tiny orchids. Down on the coast the package tourists had hardly yet begun and we could still shop and drink peacefully in the small core of what had once been a fishing village, now surrounded and submerged by concrete blocks of hotels, discos, supermarkets and souvenir shops. The black-clad housewives as yet still did their shopping in dark, almost hidden stores, the men as yet still sat gossiping in the bare-floored bars concealed by clicking bead curtains. The heart of the village as yet could still be heard beating before the summer blare of muzak drowned it out.

It was peaceful – a sort of stagnation really, I suppose. It soothed me, yet I was restless. I knew I ought to get back to London, find a real job to do instead of hanging round till Reggie wanted something. Yet I couldn't bring myself to leave; it was so beautiful; Pamela was my oldest friend.

I woke early one morning, just after dawn. The sky was like pearl, and I went out on to the terrace that ran the length of the house from the guest wing where I was, past the living quarters and on to Reggie's suite at the far end. Pamela's rooms were on the other side, the terrace ran right round. The air smelled of dew and grass and lemons and there wasn't a sound – until someone came in slippers out of Reggie's rooms at the far end and slapped quietly down the terrace steps to the garden below and out of sight. In the pale dawn light I could see quite well it was Paquita, the newish maid who made such wonderful paellas. And Reggie, wearing nothing but a towel slung over his bony shoulders, stood on the terrace and blew a kiss to her as she flitted away.

Thank God he was working and didn't appear all day. I don't know what I'd have done if I'd seen him earlier. Shock and fury possessed me. How could he! Tracy and Ingrid had been bad enough, blatant enough – but Paquita, a servant in his own house, and having her only a room or two away from his own wife! A maid, a servant who stank of sweat and garlic, who no doubt boasted and sniggered about him with the other servants, whose knowing eyes would also hold contempt. How could he – how *could* he! How could Pamela bear this humiliation? She had shut her eyes to all the others, for her own reasons, but could she shut her eyes to this? A servant, in her own house?

I got through the day somehow and the evening, watching them both like a cat. Pamela looked pale and strained, pleaded a headache; Reggie was jaunty as usual, a cravat knotted at his stringy throat, his gaze as bold as ever, brazen, his big teeth grinning. 'Ruth Ellis,' he said, 'that's who I'll do next. It's got everything – sex, jealousy, drink, the death penalty. You might turn up the cuttings, Dinah, when you go back – I know it all, of course, I was at the trial, and I've got photocopies of all the evidence. I shall get right inside the woman and her bunch of sleazy lovers, show what made them tick. The pub where she shot him's still there, of course, I knew it well at the time . . .' He went on like this and we listened. Then we went to bed.

Sex, jealousy, drink perhaps – they all lay smashed at the foot of the terrace next morning when the gardener raised the alarm. Reggie was wearing pyjamas this time, and he was dead.

The Spanish police are different from ours – very suave, very courteous, almost military in style. They waited until Pamela felt able to speak to them later that morning, when the tears had stopped, the sedative begun to work, and she was dressed, pale but calm. I sat beside her but she would not hold my hand, her fingers clenched and moving over a handkerchief. The officer explained to us what had happened: Señor Tyrrell had apparently been standing by the parapet of the terrace outside his bedroom at approximately 2 a.m. (accord-

61

ing to the police doctor). He had a glass of whisky in his hand (the fragments were shattered round his body) and had consumed a fair amount during the preceding hours. He had also perhaps consumed one or two of the sleeping pills found at his bedside . . . 'Did Señor Tyrrell take sleeping pills, señora?'

Pamela nodded. 'Sometimes – when he was on a book. He found it hard to unwind.'

'So. He is drinking quite heavily during the evening, he takes the pills, goes out on to the terrace because perhaps still insomniac, takes perhaps another pill, takes certainly some more whiskey. He stands by the parapet, he becomes dizzy from the alcohol and the drug, he falls. In falling, I fear to say, he takes with him one of the heavy pots of geraniums that stand along the terrace, and it is that, crashing upon him, which – forgive me, señora – causes your husband's death. The fall alone, possibly not – many injuries, yes, but perhaps not fatal. The geranium pot, so full, so massive – by the will of God, yes.'

She began to cry. He regarded her with soft, lively black eyes. 'I will leave you now. There will be some formalities but nothing that need distress you too much, I think. My sincere condolences, señora – he was a distinguished member of our welcome foreign community.' He got to his feet, then paused. 'Only one small thing puzzles me. How did that pot of geraniums come to fall *upon* him rather than *with* him? But there . . .' He smiled, showing an astonishing gold tooth, 'we shall no doubt find that wind and weather had made the base unstable and that he perhaps grasped it as he fell. We do not willingly wish to embarrass our foreign visitors by trifles of this kind. *Adios*, señora, and courage.'

When he had gone we did not speak for a while. I got to my feet and went to stand by the open french window, looking out over the terrace with its bougainvillea and pots of geranium, over the falling hillside to the far rim of the sea. I heard the police cars drive away. Pamela had stopped crying.

I turned back towards her.

'I won't tell,' I said.

She looked up. She was perfectly composed again, only the redness and moisture round her eyes showing distress. Her voice was calm. 'Tell what?'

'Look, Pamela,' I came and sat down again beside her. 'I'm on your side. You were right.'

'About what?'

'To do it. He was a shit.'

The colour came up in her face, faint under the pallor. 'You mustn't say that.'

'He was. He was a shit. Conceited, selfish, a womaniser. You know that. Dragging us all into his beastly murders. It's right, it's fitting he should die by murder, ironic really, justice.'

'Murder?'

'The police won't press it. You heard what he said. They don't want scandals in the foreign colony, it's bad for tourism. We'll hear no more. But if they do come after you again, I won't say a thing. I'll absolutely deny you had any motive, any reason at all. You were right to do it, Pamela, utterly right.' I reached out and covered her hand with mine.

She looked down at them for a moment and then withdrew hers, looking up at me again with a cool, candid stare.

'Why would I want Reggie dead?' she asked.

'Why? Because he was a shit. Because of his women, the way he humiliated you, flaunted his affairs. That typist girl and Ingrid and who knows how many more. And now a servant . . .'

She said quietly, 'I didn't mind.'

'Of course you did. You couldn't not. No one would

ever believe you could just go on sitting passively and let him humiliate you as he did. You'd a right to revenge.'

She got up and moved away, then turned, leaning against the fireplace where on chilly evenings a log fire used to burn. She was completely calm.

'I liked being married to Reggie,' she said, 'I liked being Mrs Reginald Tyrrell and going to parties and meeting well-known people and living here and living in London and having money and being someone. I don't love him now like I did at first – I know he was selfish and not very nice in some ways, and all that crime and stuff sickened me often. And I didn't like some of the things he wanted me to do . . .' She blushed again, faintly, 'things in bed. I was glad when he went to other people for that. People like you.'

'Me?'

'I'm not quite a fool, Dinah. I know you've always despised me and thought I'm a nitwit. But I'm quite shrewd really, and I knew almost at once when you started sleeping with Reggie. And when he dropped you. I could see how angry you were, how ashamed and resentful, for you hadn't got anything of him, had you, while I had his name and his status and his money. I didn't want Reggie dead at all, but you did.'

There was quite a long silence after this, with us just looking at each other. Then I managed a sort of a laugh. 'What utter balls,' I said, 'As if I'd cared enough! I loathed him, I absolutely loathed him.'

'Yes,' she said, 'I know.'

There was another very long silence. I was trying to get my breath back in the same way I had tried last night when I had stood outside Reggie's french windows and steeled myself to go in. I had the perfume he liked and my hair down and only my nightgown on. I don't want to remember what I said or he said; but one of the things he said was that he'd gone past it as far as that night was concerned, no matter how much I begged, and anyway he was a bit oiled and he'd taken his sleeping pills and not even Helen of Troy or a bride in the bath could raise a flicker. I know I said, 'Only a servant, I suppose?' and I know he said something absolutely foul to me and pushed me out on to the terrace, right to the edge, and I know he had a glass in his hand and I know quite well what I decided to do, and I did it.

But it was Pamela had the motive, wasn't it, and stood to gain?

So it's stalemate really, a sort of peculiar friendship still, only it's Pamela who holds the strongest hand now. She's still Mrs Reginald Tyrrell, attractive widow of that notable criminologist, so sadly missed and so great an authority on murder and its motives. And rich with it; Reggie was exceedingly clever with money, and his books go on selling and are considered classics of their kind. Which I suppose they are.

Pamela sold the villa and we share the St John's Wood house. People often call and ask to see his Black Museum. We let them, for they're often interesting people and sometimes quite attractive.

But we usually say we don't know what some of the relics are – and that includes a shard from an earthenware flower-pot with dark marks on it that might perhaps be blood. Pamela put it there.

David Fletcher

THE SCRIBBLER'S TALE

The Chairman of the Selection Committee, Burgoyne constituency, made the position quite clear to Alan at a private interview.

'This is a safe seat, Alan. Always has been. But a safe seat damaged by scandal. That's what we've got to remember. Got to keep looking over our shoulder. So, upshot of it is, whoever we select has got to be whiter than white. Get my drift? Good. Now, I think you know where my sympathies lie, which makes it damned awkward. Once you've chosen your man, last thing you want to do is pry. So, a friendly warning, old boy. A nod and a wink, say. Any little thing, ancient history, present involvements – anything they could turn into mud. They don't even have to make it stick, Alan. That's how vulnerable we are. Just thought I'd mention it, off the record, of course. You've got time to do any . . . er . . . tidying up. Not that I'm suggesting for a moment . . .'

'No. Of course not,' Alan said. 'Thank you for mentioning it.'

'Jolly good. Then I think we can safely drink to your success, old boy. Cheers.'

'Cheers.'

There wasn't much, Alan thought. Thank God there wasn't. And she would understand. She was that sort of girl. After all, he'd put it to her, she'd never really been happy down here. And later on . . . Maybe. Possibly.

Yes, if the worst came to the worst, he could always present it as a discretionary separation, a career-necessitated hiatus, sexual relations to be resumed as soon as possible. He smiled a little at that. It was funny, but he didn't feel any regret at all. Just goes to show how unreliable the emotions are. Still, it had been fun while it lasted. He knew she'd agree and see the sense of it. After all, she'd always been a model of discretion and understanding. And then, when the Committee met in a month's time, Alan Mellon would be able to put his hand honestly on his heart and swear that he was whiter than white.

Like many authors, Miles Mellon could never resist taking his own books down from the library shelf to check how many times they had been borrowed. It was vanity, of course, but any glow of satisfaction was easily quenched by reminding himself that a borrowed book was not necessarily a read book. The really good days were those when the books – all two of them – were not on the shelves. Then he could daydream about his readers. And since the House of Commons had tardily voted in favour of a Public Lending Right, Miles argued that there was a practical value in counting the number of date stamps in the books. He could dream of pennies to come, one day.

That particular Wednesday morning, both his novels reposed on the shelf. *The Talisman* had not been taken out since last week. *A Cat Softly* bore that day's date and must, therefore, have been returned early: he hoped because the reader had read it quickly. As he was about to slip the book back on the shelf, a folded sheet of paper fluttered to the library floor. He picked it up and opened it. It was a letter, on a single sheet of headed A4 note-paper, folded twice. He would have put it back, assuming that the writer would realise that they had used it as a bookmark and return to claim it, had it not, apparently, been addressed to him. Almost guiltily, glancing around the library as he did so, he put it in his pocket.

Miles selected his allowance of four books and walked the half-mile home, thinking all the time about the letter. He had never received a fan letter in his life – he was quite convinced that that was what it must be – and the novel means of getting it to him charmed him. It argued a knowledge of authors' habits. It indicated a sort of romanticism. Obviously the borrower had read the jacket copy carefully. He knew by heart that it contained the information: 'The author lives in Hammersmith with his wife and two cats.'

Recalling that phrase burst the happy bubble of anticipated flattery. That copy ought to be amended. The author lived in Hammersmith, okay, with two demanding cats. His wife had left him almost three months ago and showed no sign of returning. He was not sure why Chris had left him. She said it was because she could not bear the financial precariousness of being a full-time writer's wife. But Miles wasn't so sure. Chris wanted a baby and he had refused on the grounds that they could not possibly afford one. Not yet. Chris thought he should get a job then, because she was, at heart, a conventional sort of girl, unlike, he thought with a sudden lifting of his spirits, the person who wrote the letter.

As soon as he reached home, he went upstairs to the small back bedroom which served as his study and, with a feeling of almost adolescent excitement, spread the letter out on the desk before him.

He read the letter several times: with embarrassment, disappointment and a growing sense of alarm. The address was printed in bold grey type and was local, although he did not know it. The handwriting was large and cursive: 'feminine' was the word that came to mind.

My Dear Miles,

In spite of everything you said, I must see you again. Just once. All right, I'm begging you. I have thought and thought about it. I do understand your position, but I can't just stop loving you to order. I know I never will. I won't mess anything up. I won't create a fuss. But I must see you once more, because there is something I have a duty to tell you. I think you will agree – although you think a clean break is best – that you owe me that. It's not such a lot to ask, is it? If only I'd been able to think clearly last night, this would not be necessary.

I'm afraid you won't come. I still have those sleeping pills, Miles. I know it's cheap to threaten you but you seem like a stranger to me suddenly and I am desperate. I must see you. I'll be here, as usual. Please, Miles. I will never ask you for anything else.

I love you,
Ellie.

The letter was undated. It was evidently not intended for him. Now it seemed stupid that he had ever thought it would be. Who would write to an author in such a chancy way? Vanity again.

His first thought was to return the letter at once to the book. Ellie, whoever she was, would certainly remember such a letter and, in time, would realise where she had mislaid it. Even if she had – and her state of mind made this seem feasible – posted an empty envelope, she would surely realise eventually and return to the library, looking for her property.

He could imagine her all too clearly. Distracted, tearful, slipping the letter into the book – perhaps consciously thinking that she would remember where she had put it because of the coincidence of her lover's and the author's Christian names – when interrupted by a ring on her lonely doorbell.

He told himself to stop. He was turning the incident, this poor girl's plight, into the material for a novel already. Just as Chris always said he did. This was real life, real distress. And if he returned the letter to the library book, anyone might see it. Since 'Miles' had not received the letter, he would not come and she might . . . Therefore he couldn't throw the letter away.

Startling the cats, Miles ran downstairs and snatched up the battered A-Z, which Chris kept with the telephone directories. His hands were shaking as he turned the pages and, with difficulty, squinting at the smallness of the print, located her address.

The only thing, the only humanitarian thing, was to return the letter to her. He would just slip it through her letter box – no explanations, nothing. And please God she hadn't taken those pills.

The address was at a block of white stucco flats, c.1930, in a quiet cul-de-sac on the borders of Hammersmith and Chiswick. There were six entrances, the numbers of the flats to which they gave access carved into the lintel. A glass and wood swing door admitted him to an anonymous common hallway, covered in marbled lino-tiles. Two doors faced each other, painted pale green and with their numbers prominently displayed. Her flat, he calculated, was on the third floor. He climbed the stairs quietly, unsure why he felt so reluctant to attract any attention. On the second floor he heard the muffled sound of a radio. The third was quite silent. At hip height each door was equipped with a small metal letter flap and knocker combined. At the last moment, he had put the letter into a plain white envelope. He took it from his inside pocket and, with his left hand, pushed the flap gently inwards, to avoid any noise. To his surprise and embarrassment, the door opened inwards. He tried to grab it, to pull it closed, but some weight, a coat perhaps, hanging on its other side, made it swing wide open. He saw a tiny hall, just large enough for one person, and beyond that a small kitchen – the connecting door was open. He contemplated dropping the letter on the floor and pulling the door shut. But she might hear the noise and come looking for this mysterious postman. Or, if she had popped out, to visit a neighbour, for instance, she might not be able to get back in. It would be better to brave it out. After all, he could explain, briefly, and then run. Neither of them need be very embarrassed. He cleared his throat.

'Hello? Excuse me. Anyone there?'

His voice echoed down the stairway. Beside the door was a bellpush. He pressed it. Silence. Obviously it didn't work. There was nothing else for it but to go in. He stepped into the hall and faced the open front door. He rattled the knocker which produced an inadequate, tinny sound.

'Oh damn it,' he muttered.

The door behind him revealed a cluttered bathroom, very feminine. He closed the door. Standing almost in the kitchen he pushed the front door to, thinking what a bloody stupid design this was, and then started as the door latched shut. He swore again. There were several coats and a dressing gown hanging on the front door, which explained why it had opened so easily. Bracing himself, he tapped on the door which was revealed by closing the front door. He tapped again, waited and then opened it.

'Excuse me. Hello?'

It was a nice airy room, comfortably furnished. Well, he decided, he would put the envelope on the table by the window and get out before someone mistook him for a burglar. On tip toe, feeling nervous and thoroughly foolish, he crossed the room and placed the letter squarely in the middle of a highly polished table, set beneath the window. He glanced out and was relieved to see the street below as deserted as when he had come in. That was that, then, he thought. And he'd never take a piece of paper from a library book again. He turned around and froze.

71

There was another door, leading into a bedroom. It was open and she was sprawled half on the bed, half off. She was dead. He could tell that from her upside down, glassy eyes, her horrible immobility. But not from sleeping pills. Not from an overdose. Her throat, the front of her white blouse were spotted with wounds. She had lost so much blood that it was only by the sleeves of the blouse that he could be sure it was white, not reddish brown.

He did not think. If he had, possibly the nightmare would never have happened. He looked around the room with a calmness of purpose which later he was to curse. Of all the times in his life not to panic . . . He located the white telephone, picked up the receiver. Quite steadily, he dialed 999.

'Well? What do you think?' Inspector Flax said, tilting his chair back.

'Charge him,' Detective Sergeant Stewart replied without hesitation.

Not for the first time, Flax marvelled at the simplicity and hardness of youth.

'Good film on the tele later, is there?' he asked, not without sarcasm since Stewart's passion for the cinema had so often caused Flax to be subjected to detailed accounts of endless plots.

'As it happens, yes. But that's not the point. What choice do you have?'

Flax forbore to point out that Miles Mellon just might be telling the truth.

'You tell me.'

'Easy. Miles Mellon, not very successful author, is having a bit on the side. Understandable since his missus walked out on him. But the girl wants something permanent. And Mellon wants his wife back, badly. Sunday night, he gives the girl her marching orders. She seems to go along with it. Too stunned to do anything else. Monday, she calls in sick, writes Mellon the letter and posts it on her way to the library. Tuesday, Mellon answers the letter in person. She makes difficulties. She's not prepared just to fade away. Mellon loses his temper and does for her, dumping the knife in the river on the way home, or somebody's dustbin. At home, he settles down to sweat it out. Wednesday afternoon, he can't take any more. He gets curious. There's been no word about her on the radio, nothing in the papers. He goes to have a little look-see. Then he decides it's better all out in the open. He makes up the tale of finding the letter, rings us and hey presto. Clever. Very clever. But not clever enough.'

'How did he get in? She couldn't open the door and he doesn't have a key.'

'Or he did have a key but he's dumped it. Or, he used the one under the dustbin in the cubbyhole beside the front door.'

'Check that for prints.'

'Already being done, sir. Meanwhile we have his dabs on the door, bathroom door, table, phone . . .'

'Why did she return her library books early?'

'She'd finished them.'

'Why didn't she take others out?'

'Didn't feel like reading? Understandable under the circs. Or perhaps she was planning to leave, if she could persuade Mellon to pay her off.'

'We'll see,' Flax said, and stood up.

'You don't buy it?'

'I'm not as convinced as you.'

'He has no alibi,' Stewart protested. 'Sat at home reading, watching the box. Anyone can check what's on TV . . .'

'Well, we'll hang on to him. See what tomorrow brings. If you're a good boy, you might even get home in time to see the film.'

*

73

The next morning, Inspector Flax had a lot more information. Miss Ellen (Ellie) Hankin had rented the flat barely three months before. She was a civil servant who had come to London because the transfer she had requested months before had finally been granted. It had been a small step up the ladder.

Mrs Anne Graze, civil servant, colleague of the deceased:

'There was definitely a man in her life. She admitted as much, but, of course, I didn't like to pry. I got the impression he was married, but she definitely had hopes. She said to me once, if it hadn't been for an attachment, "for the chance of happiness", she would never have come to London. But she was cagey about him. I'd said to her once, because I felt quite sorry for her, you know, perhaps she'd like to come to supper, with Ron and me, and bring her friend. She said that wouldn't be possible. She'd like to but, well, she knew I'd understand. Well, what else could I think but that he was married and they were having to be careful?'

Mrs Suzanne Poulter, neighbour:

'She was very quiet and very clean. Always wrapped her rubbish in newspaper. The bins get so smelly. Honestly, you wouldn't believe what some people put in them, and all naked for the eye to see. But not Miss Hankin. She was a good neighbour. Quiet, clean and kept herself to herself. Visitors? Well, I'm not nosy so I couldn't say for sure but as far as I know, she only had one regular visitor. Yes. A gentleman. Well, yes, I think I could recognise him, but he always wore a hat and I only ever saw him on the stairs. Just a glimpse. Well, yes, once or twice in the street. Yes, from my window. I just happened to be glancing out. You know, the way you do. No. Always on foot. We're only a few minutes from the tube, you see. Very convenient.'

Flax had a Constable equipped with a photograph of

Miles Mellon and told him to show it to everyone living in the cul-de-sac.

'Pathologist's report, sir,' Stewart said, grinning.
    'Anything interesting?'
    'Nothing, except that she was three months pregnant.'

'Look, why don't you make it easy on yourself? Where did you dump the knife?'
    'I didn't dump the knife. I didn't kill her.'
    'When did you last see her?'
    'I told you, I only ever saw her once . . . when I phoned you.'
    'Why did your wife leave you, Mr Mellon?'
    'Because she felt insecure. She wanted me to take a full-time job whereas I thought – I've got another book coming out and the publisher is hopeful – I thought I'd be able to make it doing what I want to do.'
    'I thought you said your wife wanted a family?'
    'Yes, but we couldn't afford . . .'
    'So you wouldn't be able to afford Ellie Hankin's baby, either. When did she tell you, Mellon? The night you killed her?'
    'She never told me, I . . .'
    'That's what she had to tell you, wasn't it? Well, we'll go into that later. Your brother's here. I'll send him in, all right?'

Although he was a little over six feet tall, Alan Mellon could not see out of the single window in the room: it was placed too high.
    'Thank you for coming,' Miles said, wishing he would sit down.
    'It was the least I could do, though . . .'
    'Yes?'

75

'How's Chris taking it?'

'I don't know. They only allowed me one phone call . . .'

'And you used it to call me?'

'I didn't know what else to do. I thought you'd know someone . . . a lawyer . . .'

'It couldn't have come at a worse time, Miles. It's a very difficult time for me . . .'

'I'm innocent. I never knew this woman. You've got to believe me.'

'More to the point, do the police believe you?'

'I don't know. They said something about an identification parade.'

'Best to go along with them. Nothing like being co-operative . . .'

'Look, do you know a lawyer, a good one?'

'Yes.'

'Will you get him for me?'

'Well, of course, I *can* . . .'

'*Will* you?'

Alan hesitated, moistening his lips.

'Of course. It's the very least I can do.'

'Thank you.'

'Anything else?'

'No. And it's all right, Alan. I am innocent. You won't be . . . embarrassed.'

'Of course not.'

Later, Miles stood in line with eleven other men in the yard behind the police station. They had given him a rather battered trilby and told him to put it on. Six of the men wore hats, trilbies, caps, a lone pork-pie: the others were bareheaded.

Mrs Suzanne Poulter, swathed in astrakhan, walked briskly along the line. In a silence which struck Miles as ominous, she touched him on the right shoulder.

Mr Arnold Pearce, who occupied the ground floor

76

flat opposite that of the deceased, walked up and down
the line hesitantly. He interrupted his fourth journey,
right to left, to peer into Miles's flushed face. Then he
touched him on the right shoulder.

Afterwards, he told Inspector Flax that he was
almost a hundred per cent sure. It was just that the man
he had seen going in and out of Ellie Hankin's block,
whom he had recognised from the photograph the
Constable had shown him, had seemed taller than the
man on the line.

'Oh nonsense, Mr Pearce,' Mrs Poulter said firmly.
'I've been much closer to him than you. *I* live on the
same landing. That's him, no doubt about it. Being so
small myself, I'd have been sure to notice if he was a tall
man. No, that's him. Absolutely no question. You
know, Inspector, I always thought there was something
shifty about him.'

Miles was charged with murder half an hour later and
then left alone with his lawyer.

'Mr Mellon? Robert Shore.'

Miles took his hand automatically. He could not
believe that any of this was happening. He became
aware of the man's stare.

'What is it?' he said.

'I'm so sorry. The resemblance to your brother . . .
Quite remarkable.'

'Oh. Listen, what can you do for me?'

'Only my best. But I can promise you that. After
all, the brother of a future MP, a man tipped for a
junior ministry at the very least . . . My best, I promise
you.'

'You do realise I'm innocent?'

'Of course, my dear fellow. Only there are some
rather damning circumstances. Still, obstacles are
meant to be overcome, don't you agree? Shall we
sit?'

*

77

'What did the wife say?' Stewart looked tired. He pulled off his raincoat and hung it on the peg next to Flax's.

'Nothing much. What about you?'

'All here.' He slapped a sheaf of typed pages on Flax's desk.

'Save my eyesight,' the Inspector invited, tilting his chair back.

'Parents first, then. Thoroughly respectable girl. Left home two years ago but kept in touch. No boy friends, which up there is considered not only laudable but earns her a gold star in the family bible.'

'So if there was someone and he was married, she'd probably keep very quiet about it.' Stewart nodded agreement. 'But damn it, there must have been someone . . .'

'Two. One now married. One overseas. Middle-East, we think. Her sister says neither of 'em were serious. The one I talked to, the married one, confirms. Says she wouldn't.'

'Wouldn't what?'

'Screw.'

'Oh.'

'But the sister says there was somebody. About a year ago. Ellie changed. Rosy cheeks. A glint in her eye. Week-ends away. A holiday. The sister is certain there was a man. Supposed he was married. Ellie hinted he was in the public eye.'

'That would fit Mellon.'

'Sort of.'

'What about the week-ends, the holiday?'

Stewart shrugged.

'She never let on, did she?'

'What about girl friends?'

'It's in the report. Nobody close. Nobody with any hard information. But, like everyone else, they're sure there was a man and supposed he must be married.'

'The ideal mistress,' Flax sighed. 'Discreet, available, pretty and close.'

'But pregnant. That's not ideal. Now, what about the wife?'

'She backs Mellon up. No suspicion of a mistress. Thought had never crossed her mind.'

'But?'

'She conceded he could have taken up with somebody after she left. He likes his oats, our Mellon. Apparently.'

'Who doesn't?' Stewart said. 'Which reminds me, any chance of calling it a night, sir?'

'A girl?'

'Brigitte Bardot on the telly.'

'When did you meet her, Mellon?'

'I didn't. I've told you and told you . . .'

'It was before your wife left, wasn't it? You went to Yorkshire three times in the last year.'

'That's right.'

'Twice you were tutor on a writing course . . .'

'You can check.'

'We have. And the third time . . .'

'Lectured a writing circle.'

'Only one night.'

'I stayed a week. I went walking. It helps me think.'

'You realise, of course, that on all these occasions you were never further than thirty miles from Ellie Hankin's home town?'

'Sure. Except I didn't know it was her home town. I didn't know her.'

'These week-ends away . . .'

'To work. Sometimes I needed just to get away, out of London. You can check.'

'We have.'

'Well, then.'

'You could have been at this cottage of your

brother's. He agrees he lent it to you. But it's a pretty remote sort of place, isn't it, Mellon? You could have had a girl there, easy. A discreet girl. Nobody would have been any the wiser.'

'But I didn't.'

'What name did she use?'

'Pardon?'

'In Bath. We've got your name in the hotel register but we can't find hers.'

'That's because she wasn't there.'

'Stayed somewhere else, did she? Afternoon nookie? Sneak her up the back stairs, did you?'

'I never, ever in my life slept with Ellie Rankin.'

'Somebody did.'

'Then find the bastard and charge him.'

Alan Mellon met Robert Shore at his club.

'Sorry about the newspapers,' Shore said. 'There was very little I could do.'

'I understand. What's the position now?'

'I'll be frank with you, Alan. It looks bad. In fact, I've advised your brother to plead guilty. I think we could get somewhere with a plea of diminished responsibility, balance of the mind and all that, but he won't hear of it, I'm afraid.'

Alan said nothing. He tapped with his fingers on the arm of the leather chair.

'There's not a shred of evidence to support his story. Worse, there's nothing to link the deceased with another man.'

'You're sure?' Alan asked, his voice taking on a note of urgency. 'You've checked yourself?'

'Not personally. But my men are the very best. And the police have been exceedingly thorough. If there was anything, I assure you we would have found it.'

'Amazing.'

'I beg your pardon?'

'Miles. Amazing that he could have . . . You are absolutely certain?'

'I very much regret that I am. Unless you could persuade him . . . ?'

'No. He wouldn't listen to me. We've never been close. Besides I . . . I can say this to you, Robert. I know you'll understand. I'm up for formal adoption as the Burgoyne candidate next week. It's been indicated to me that I should keep my distance until then.'

'Oh quite. Well . . . I hope I needn't say how sorry I am?'

'Thank you.'

'We'll do our best, of course. But it would be wrong of me not to tell you that I expect a conviction.'

'I'm only sorry I involved you in a hopeless case.'

'Oh, to lose one now and again does no harm. Shows you're not infallible. Judges like that.'

'Chris? You do believe me, don't you?'

'Of course I . . . Oh, Miles, look . . . If you . . . Well, I can't say I wouldn't mind. Of course I would. But if you were to change your mind . . . about the plea . . . I would try to understand.'

'Chris . . . I didn't know the woman. I didn't kill her. I know it sounds crazy, all of it, but I . . .'

'All right, Miles. I believe you. Of course I do.'

Her voice was as hollow as the bang of his cell door at lock-up time.

When, almost a week later, Robert Shore received a message from Miles Mellon requesting an immediate interview, he dared to hope that his client had seen reason at last. After all, speaking personally, he didn't *like* to lose. And then the waste of taxpayer's money, when a simple plea of guilty . . . He greeted Miles expectantly.

'Look, there's something I've remembered. Something I want you to look into.'

'Of course, my dear fellow. Any scraps, no matter how small . . . at this stage . . . gratefully received and all that.' Shore was fairly certain he had managed to keep the disappointment out of his voice.

'I'd better warn you it's going to sound crazy. As crazy as everything else.'

'Let me be the judge of that, will you? Now, calmly. Take your time.' He fixed his grey eyes on the wall behind and above Miles's head. Miles told himself not to be paranoid: of course Shore wasn't bored.

'Years ago – I can't remember when exactly. Before I was married. I think when I'd just come down from University. Alan might remember. Anyway, I wrote a story. I was always writing but this particular story, well, I thought it had possibilities. Look, the point is, this story was about a man who had a very rich wife. He also had a mistress. She was very quiet, discreet, and he was painstakingly careful. Nobody, but nobody knew about them. The girl didn't even know the man's real name. He used a friend's. Then the girl became demanding. She wanted marriage. He couldn't do without his wife's money – he'd got used to it, you see – so he killed the girl. And the idea was, you see, that the friend, the one whose name he'd used, was mistaken for the murderer.'

'I'm sorry, but I don't see what you're trying to tell me.'

'The idea. Don't you see? Only I couldn't finish the story. I couldn't work out how the man could implicate his friend.'

'And what happened to this story?'

Miles looked down at the table, his hands clenched.

'I gave it to Alan. He was always good at puzzles, logic, that sort of thing. I asked him if he could think of an ending.'

'And?' Shore sounded cautious

'He couldn't.' Miles glanced up at him. 'He gave it back to me. He couldn't solve it either.'

Shore said:

'Where is this story now?'

'I'm not sure. I can't remember. I might have thrown it away. I do that sometimes.'

'No one else read it?'

'That's just it. Alan might have lent it to someone and then . . .'

Shore stood up.

'I think I get your drift, Mr Mellon. However, I can't believe that you mean me to draw any implications from this.'

'If you'd just ask Alan . . . ask him if he showed it to anyone. If he remembers it.'

'I'll do that if you really wish it.'

'I don't believe in coincidences. Somebody read that story and thought up an end and then . . .'

'I really do think — and please forgive my bluntness — a plea of diminished responsibility would stand a very good chance. I could arrange for you to see a psychiatrist . . .'

'No. I'm not mad,' Miles shouted, hitting the table. Shore looked coldly offended by this show of emotion. Miles forced himself to be calm. 'If you'll just ask Alan. Ask him if he showed it to anyone.'

'As you know he's away. Next week, I'll do what I can. Now, if there's nothing else?'

Miles shook his head.

Robert Shore did not ask Alan Mellon about the story. He felt it would be too embarrassing, that Alan could only draw one implication from it and that, of course, was unthinkable. Besides, Shore had a flourishing career to consider. The friendship of an MP, a future junior minister, was not to be put in jeopardy, certainly

83

not for the delusions of a patently guilty man. Had there
been the slightest possibility of it being in Miles's
interest, naturally he would have placed his client
above all other considerations. As it was, since he was
batting on a losing wicket, he owed it to himself to
ensure that Alan Mellon would have good reason to
field the ball at some future stage. No, there was
absolutely no point in putting it to Alan. Poor Miles was
obviously off his rocker.

The Chairman of the Selection Committee, Burgoyne
constituency, made the position apologetically clear to
Alan at a private interview.

'Terribly sorry, Alan. Commiserations and all that.
Know how you must feel. Damned rotten luck. This
business with your brother was the clincher. I did warn
you . . .'

'There was nothing I could do.'

'No. 'Course not. But mud, Alan. Any breath of
scandal . . . Absolutely not on at this point in time. And
word has it he doesn't stand a cat in hell's chance. Still,
Melhuish is a good man. Not as able as you, of course,
but clean, Alan. Absolutely beyond reproach. Still, I'm
damned sorry. But there'll be an election in three years,
vacant seats. The dust will have settled by then. Perhaps sooner. Another by-election. Never know your
luck. So, don't be too down in the mouth, eh?'

'No.'

'Sorry for your brother, too, poor beggar. He was a
scribbler they tell me.'

'Yes.'

'Hmm. Always thought that sort of person was . . .
well . . . bit unreliable, you know. Still, rotten luck on
you.'

'Well, mixed,' Alan said and managed a faint smile.

'That's the spirit. Look for a silver lining. Needless to

say, once the dust's settled, I'll put in a word. After all, poor beggar can't be charged twice, can he?'

'No,' said Alan. 'And thank you.'

'Least I could do. Oh and Alan . . . Now that you won't be standing, there'd be no harm in making a bit of a show at the trial. Family solidarity and all that.'

'Yes. I owe him that anyway,' Alan said, and meant it.

Michael Gilbert

AUDITED AND FOUND CORRECT

At the offices of Messrs Maybury and Goodnight, Solicitors, the order of departure was an established ritual. It varied only when Mr Goodnight left early, as he usually did: in the summer for a game of golf or in the winter for a meeting of one of the many societies in which he was interested.

When he was not there Sal and Beth started at five o'clock packing up their typewriters and tidying their desks. They would be away by a quarter past five, closely followed, and occasionally preceded by young Mr Manifold, the articled clerk. At five-thirty the litigation clerk, Mr Prince, and the conveyancing clerk, Mr Dallow, left, though not together since they had not been on speaking terms for two years.

There remained only Sergeant Pike, late of the Royal Marine Corps, who had the job of locking up; and Mr Prosper, the cashier.

As the girls hurried past on the pavement they could look down into the lighted semi-basement room where Mr Prosper sat at his work. They used to make jokes about him. He was a bachelor who lived by himself, so people said, in a small North London flat.

'Not much to go home to,' said Sal. 'No wonder he stays late.'

'When does he go home, anyway?' said Beth. 'I had to come back once, for something I'd left behind. It was after seven. He was still at it.'

'Perhaps he stays there all night,' said Sal.

They had a giggle about this.

'Poor old boy,' said Beth. She was the warmer-hearted of the two. 'What a life, eh? Adding up and subtracting and that sort of thing all day long.'

'He chose it,' said Sal. 'If he's bloody miserable, it's his own fault, isn't it?' Sal was the cynic.

They were both wrong.

Mr Prosper was not miserable. He was happy. He had a job which suited him precisely and he would have asked for none other.

Since childhood he had been fascinated by figures. He could add and subtract before he could spell. He liked arranging figures, setting them out in orderly columns, correcting and adjusting them, comparing the totals he arrived at. He compared primes and cube roots as another boy might have compared birds' eggs or stamps.

If his mind had been of a more theoretical bent he might have become a qualified accountant. It was a step he had considered more than once, but rejected. It was the figures themselves which interested him, not the intricacies of taxation and company law which he would have had to master to become an accountant. He was happy to be a bookkeeper and a cashier. That was his métier.

He had joined Messrs Maybury and Goodnight thirty-five years before, when Alfred Maybury was alive and Richard Goodnight was quite a young man. He had watched over its fortunes from the earliest days, when no one knew where the next week's wages were coming from, until the happy moment when they had acquired Jim Collard as a client. At that time Jim, who was now boss of the Collard Empire of shops and offices, had been at the beginning of *his* career. Richard Goodnight had done a job for him, and done it well. Their company work went, of course, to a large City firm, but all the conveyancing and much of the day-to-day contract work and debt collecting, inseparable from Collard enterprises, came to them.

Mr Prosper worried about it sometimes. He said to Sergeant Pike, who was his only confidant in such matters, 'We're a one-man firm with a one-man client.'

'Should last out our time,' said Pike. 'And old Goodnight's.'

'He'll take in young Manifold, as soon as he's qualified.'

'Don't care for him,' said Pike. 'Too much grease on his hair.'

They neither of them cared for Manifold, who had been to a famous public school, and wore the knowledge of it like a badge in the button-hole of his well-cut suit.

'Ought to be in some large outfit,' said Pike. 'Doesn't fit here.'

The smallness of the firm was an added attraction to Mr Prosper. In a larger organisation he would have had assistants. He would have been forced to delegate. Here, he could keep his eye on everything. Once a year a qualified accountant was called in to audit his books, for the satisfaction of the watchdogs at the Law Society. He had an easy task. 'I wish they were all like yours,' he used to say. 'Never a record mislaid or a penny missing.'

The early evening was Mr Prosper's favourite time. His papers, like good children, were all in bed, tucked up in their folders. Perhaps he might have, on the desk in front of him, a single sheet of foolscap ruled in double columns on which he would be making some last minute calculations, or he might be reconciling the client balances or adjusting the PAYE records. An adjustment and reconciliation which was entirely superfluous. But only part of his mind would be on the job. His real thoughts were running down other tracks.

It was his habit, during such moments of agreeable

relaxation, to weigh up his colleagues and acquaintances, their achievements and failures, their gains and losses, just as though they were business enterprises, each with his own personal balance sheet, which he himself was charged with the job of inspecting.

How would Richard Goodnight come out of such an audit?

There were undeniable items on the debit side. He did a minimum of work to justify the profits of the firm which, since Mr Maybury's death, came into his hands alone. Mr Prosper knew little about his private life, but was aware that he had a flat near Sloane Square, a house in the country, and shares in a shooting syndicate in Kent and fishing in Scotland. He seemed to change his car every year.

Nor was his day an onerous one. His average time of arrival over the past six months had been 10.27. His average time of departure 4.59. Subtract from this an average lunch hour of one hour and fifty-two minutes, and this left a working day of four hours and forty minutes, during which he saw a few old clients and dictated a few letters.

The real work of the firm was done by Mr Prince and Mr Dallow.

On the credit side, Mr Prosper conceded, there were two balancing items. First, the fact that if anything did go really wrong – and the number of things which could go wrong with a one-man solicitor's firm were legion – the disaster would fall upon Mr Goodnight alone. The rest of them would lose their jobs. He would lose all that he possessed. Again, credit had to be given for his share in setting up the firm, his part in the early struggles and the fact that Sam Collard's work, on which the firm depended, had come through him. Yes, his account was roughly in balance.

At the other end of the scale, take Sergeant Pike. There were substantial, if imponderable assets on the credit side of *his* balance sheet. Twenty years of service in the Marines. The confidence which his record inspired. (Three firms had competed for him when he left the Service.) Excellent health. The financial security of his pension. Yes. A lot of pluses there and very few minuses.

In contrast, what could be said for young Manifold? Too much grease in his hair, Pike had said. Too much grease all round, thought Mr Prosper. He had been given his articles in the firm, in preference to a number of abler young men, simply because he was Sam Collard's nephew. He did the simplest work, and made mistakes which even the girls laughed at. All he seemed interested in was playing games. Indeed, thought Mr Prosper, he spent a great deal more time in squash and racquets courts than he did in the law courts; and for these inconsiderable services he was paid rather more than Sergeant Pike and almost as much as Mr Prosper himself. Moreover it was clear from his conduct and his manner that he already saw himself as future head of the firm.

It was at this point that the well-sharpened pencil in Mr Prosper's hand checked for a moment, moved on, checked again, and then went back.

The task to which he had been devoting himself that evening was his periodical check of disbursement books. These were records, kept by everyone in the firm, of the petty cash which they expended in the course of their duties; fares, searches, commissioners' fees and the like. They were operated on a simple in-and-out system. You paid the money out of your own pocket, noted it in your book, and recovered what was owing to you at the end of the week.

The disbursement book in front of him belonged to young Manifold, and the item at which his pencil had checked was dated September 20th. It said 'Collards. Purchase of shop 220 Holloway Road. Taxis £3.80.'

Mr Prosper climbed stiffly to his feet, went out into the passage, and made his way along to Manifold's room. Papers on the table, papers on the window ledge, papers on the floor.

'No idea of system and order,' said Mr Prosper. It took him some minutes to locate the file he wanted in the bottom drawer of one of the cabinets. He sat down to study it. The solicitors acting for the owners of that particular shop had been Blumfeldts, and it was at their offices, at the far end of Holborn, that the purchase would have been completed.

'Ten minutes' walk, five minutes in a bus,' said Mr Prosper.

The memory which had stopped him was of something he had overheard Sal saying to Beth. 'Guess what, I came back in the bus with Prince Andrew last Thursday, and he paid my fare.'

Last Thursday had been September 20th and Prince Andrew was the name which the girls had bestowed on young Manifold. It was possible, of course, that the bus trip had been unconnected with the completion of 220 Holloway Road, but in any event £3.80 was an incredible amount for a taxi fare to and from the end of Holborn.

Collards were always buying and selling small shop and office properties, and after the conveyancing work had been done by Mr Dallow it would have been normal for the routine job of completing the purchase, paying over the money and collecting the deeds to be entrusted to the articled clerk. There were a dozen files in the cabinet which related to such transactions.

Panting slightly with the exertion Mr Prosper gathered them up, and left the room.

In the passage he encountered Sergeant Pike, who said, 'Let me carry those for you.'

'Quite all right,' said Mr Prosper breathlessly. 'I can manage.'

It annoyed him that the slightest exertion made him puff and wheeze.

Back in his own room he spread the files on his desk and started to read them. From time to time he referred back from a file to the disbursement book. Now that his suspicions had been aroused it was only too easy to detect the signs of small but systematic cheating that had been going on.

In one case completion had been postponed at the last moment, from Friday in one week until Wednesday in the week following. Manifold had claimed taxi expenses for *both* occasions. Then there were the local search fees. Search fees had to be paid, of course, but there seemed to be altogether too many of them. An analysis of the transactions that Manifold had been engaged in over the last six months showed thirteen purchases, eleven sales and no fewer than sixty fees. Mr Prosper's pencil scurried across a fresh sheet of paper, analysing, computing, comparing.

Sergeant Pike pushed his head in and said, 'I'm off. I'll leave the front door on the latch. Bang it as you go out.' He spotted the pile of files and peered at the notes Mr Prosper was making.

'Has our golden boy been putting his foot in it again?'

'Yes,' said Mr Prosper. 'I really think he has.'

He was a man who liked to take his time and move slowly. He needed incontrovertible proof.

Next morning he had a word with Sal. He realised that one member of the staff would be unlikely to incriminate another, and he had to proceed with craft.

Fortunately he had found, in the girl's own disbursement book, an item for a single bus fare to the Bank of England dated September 20th, and described, in her school girl writing, as 'Documents by hand'.

He said to her, 'I've been checking these books. Surely you've been undercharging. Why only a single bus fare? Did you walk back?'

Sal thought about it, and said, 'No, that's quite right. Thursday afternoon, Mr Manifold paid my fare. He got on at St Paul's. We came back together.'

'Ah, that accounts for it,' said Mr Prosper, handing her back the book. It did, in fact, account for it. The completion had been that afternoon. Blumfeldt's office was within a stone's throw of St Paul's.

His next call was on Mr Dallow, a precise and solemn man with the air of an undertaker. He said, 'I've been looking through these disbursement books, and I've been puzzled by all these references to local search fees. Could you explain about that.'

'I usually get the articled clerk to do the local searches. Something wrong with them?'

'Nothing wrong, no. I wondered if you could explain. Just exactly what *are* local search fees? How many do you have to make?'

'That depends. Normally, one Borough Council and one County Council. If you're dealing with a County Borough, of course, you only have to make one search.'

'I see,' said Mr Prosper. He had been wondering whether it would be safe to take Mr Dallow fully into his confidence. He decided to do so. Mr Dallow was the soul of discretion.

He pushed the disbursement book across. Mr Dallow cast an eye down the entries, and uttered a series of 'tuts' and 'tchks' like an electric kettle coming to the boil.

He said, 'This is nonsense, absolute nonsense. Purchase of Malpas House. Three search fees! Why, that sale never went through at all. It was cancelled before it even started. And what's this? Six separate searches for 3, 5 and 7 Caxton House. They're all flats in the same block, and St Alban's is a County Borough. One search would have covered the lot. What's the boy playing at?'

'I should hardly describe it as "play",' said Mr Prosper coldly.

'And why wasn't it picked up in the bill?'

'It wasn't picked up,' said Mr Prosper, 'because they were all Collard's transactions. Instead of sending them a separate bill for each one, as we should do, we debit them quarterly with all their costs for the last three months. I've often pointed out to Mr Goodnight that this was a slack and dangerous way of doing business and likely to lead to errors.'

'Which it has.'

'Not errors, Dallow. Systematic fraud.'

'We shall have to tell Mr Goodnight.'

'I'd rather you said nothing about it until I've had a word with Manifold. He might have some explanation.'

But Mr Prosper did not say this as though he believed it.

In the luncheon interval he left a note on Manifold's desk, *I would like to see you about your disbursement book. Please look in at 5.30 this evening. J.P.*

'Well,' said Manifold. 'So what's it all about? I hope it's not going to take too long. I've got a court booked for six o'clock.'

He indicated the handle of the squash racquet sticking out of the top of his brief case. He did not seem at all apprehensive.

'How long it takes depends entirely on you,' said Mr Prosper. He had the offending disbursement book on the desk in front of him, and had marked a dozen places in it with slips of paper. 'I'd like an explanation, if there is an explanation, of some of these sums of money you've been claiming.'

'What do you mean, explanation? They're my petty cash expenses. Fares and so on.'

'Money you've actually spent.'

Manifold looked at him for a long moment, and then burst into laughter. It had quite a genuine ring about it. 'You've been snooping,' he said. He picked up the book and started to look at the entries which Mr Prosper had marked. Occasionally he chuckled. 'Quite a neat bit of detection,' he said, 'but you've missed one or two. Those commissioners' fees – £4.20. That was a bit of a try on. And a couple of extra taxi fares there.'

Mr Prosper was almost speechless. At last he managed to say, 'Do I understand that you admit it?'

'Fiddling the petty cash? Of course I admit it. Everyone does it.'

'I beg your pardon,' said Mr Prosper. 'Everyone does *not* do it. Not in a decent, honest, old-fashioned firm like this.'

'Old-fashioned is right,' said Manifold, looking round Mr Prosper's basement room, with its wooden cabinets, black deed boxes and solid furniture. 'Dickensian is the word that occurs to me. I think it's time we caught up with the twentieth century.'

Mr Prosper said, picking his words carefully, 'Nineteenth, twentieth or twenty-first century, it makes no difference. Honesty is still honesty, and dishonesty is dishonesty.'

'And realism is realism,' said Manifold. He had perched himself on the corner of the desk, and seemed to have forgotten the urgency of his appointment on the squash court. 'Have you ever worked out exactly what the effect of a transaction like that is?' He tapped the disbursement book. 'The effect on the client, I mean.'

'The effect is, that if he knew about it, he'd realise he was being cheated.'

'You're still not thinking about this realistically. Look. Suppose I help myself to £100 in this way. Everything I claim appears as an item in the Collard Company bill. Right?'

Mr Prosper said nothing.

'It's an expense, and allowable for tax in the accounts of the company. Corporation tax at 52%. Then the profits of the company pay tax and surtax when they come into Uncle Jim's hands. Do you know, he once told me that for every hundred pounds that goes in at the bottom, he can only count on touching ten pounds when it comes out at the top?'

Mr Prosper still said nothing.

'Work it out for yourself. If I asked Uncle Jim for a hundred pounds – which I'm sure he'd be very happy to give me – it would cost him a thousand quid to raise it. Right? If, on the other hand, I work it this way, it costs him ten pounds, and the Chancellor of the Exchequer provides the other ninety, and loses nine hundred into the bargain.'

His face white, his mouth compressed to a thin line, Mr Prosper said, 'Fraud is fraud, however you wrap it up.'

Manifold got up off the desk. As he did so, Mr Prosper realised that he was a large and athletic young man, twice as big and twice as strong as he was himself. It also occurred to him that they might be alone in the building. Sergeant Pike sometimes got away early, leaving him to lock the street door. However, he had no intention of climbing down. He waited for Manifold's answer, which came in a very different way from the light and chaffing tone he had employed up to that point.

He said, 'What are you going to do about it?'

'I shall report it.'

'Who to?'

'Mr Goodnight.'

'And what do you suppose he'll do about it?'

'Inform the Law Society and have your articles cancelled.'

'He won't.'

'He'll have no option.'

'He won't do it, for two good reasons. The first is, that if he did so, he'd lose all the Collard work. I'd guarantee that.'

96

Mr Prosper looked at him with loathing.

'The second reason is, that if old Goodnight starts stirring up trouble, he may find it bounces. Have you ever wondered why you don't look after his private tax? Why he handles it all himself?'

'What are you getting at?'

'How do you imagine he lives at the rate he does? Two houses, two cars, an expensive wife, shooting, fishing. He's been fiddling his tax for years. And the best of British luck to him.'

By this time Mr Prosper was profoundly shocked and almost speechless. If Manifold had cut short the interview at this point, the worst might not have occurred. Unfortunately, he changed gear, and said, with an unhappy assumption of bonhomie, 'Come along old chap, don't be an ass. Forget the whole thing.'

Mr Prosper took a deep breath, and said, 'No.'

'You're determined to make a fuss?' Manifold's mouth hardened. 'You'd risk your job, and the jobs of everyone else here, for a few pounds that no one cares about, least of all the man who's paying it?'

'I won't be blackmailed into being accessory to a fraud.'

'I imagine,' said Manifold with calculated brutality, 'that other people here will be able to find themselves jobs. The typists and Sergeant Pike, and so on. But one thing I'm sure about, and that is that you won't.'

'Insolence won't help you.'

'You're not only stupid, you're old-fashioned. You're out of date. People like you aren't needed any more.'

Anger was having its way with Mr Prosper now. A red-hot, scalding anger that drove out fear.

'That job you're doing, counting on your fingers, it can be done by any school leaver with a pocket calculator. You're not just out of date. You're obsolete.'

Mr Prosper was on his feet now. His groping fingers touched the heavy round ruler on his desk and closed on

97

it. He took two steps towards the astonished Manifold and swung a blow, downwards, at his head.

Manifold had no difficulty at all in avoiding it. His reactions were twice as fast as Mr Prosper's. He jumped back nimbly. The blow fell on thin air. Mr Prosper overbalanced and collapsed, hitting his head on the corner of the desk as he went down. As he did so the ruler shot out of his hand and hit Manifold on the shin.

Manifold laughed, picked up the ruler, and said, 'Watch it old boy. You'll be hurting someone.'

He was struck by the way Mr Prosper was lying and went down on to one knee beside him. He said, 'Come along, get up off the floor.'

The arm he was holding felt curiously limp.

A sound made him jerk his head round. Sergeant Pike was standing in the doorway. He said, 'You'd better get hold of a doctor, Sergeant. Mr Prosper's had a fall.'

Sergeant Pike came over, pushed Manifold roughly out of the way, and knelt beside Mr Prosper. After a long moment he got up, walked across the room, and locked the door, pocketing the key. Then he picked up the telephone and started to dial.

Manifold said, 'What are you doing.'

'I'm calling the police,' said Sergeant Pike.

Cosmo Franks deployed the case for the Crown with the dispassionate care which is expected of Senior Treasury Counsel.

In answer to his questions, Mr Dallow told the Court that the deceased had been on the point of exposing a systematic series of frauds by the accused. Sergeant Pike spoke of hearing a crash, coming into the room and finding the accused bending over the body. He had been holding a heavy wooden ruler in his hand and had put it down as the Sergeant came through the door. An officer from the Forensic Science Laboratory said that the fingerprints of the accused were on the ruler. The only surprise was the medical evidence.

Dr Summerson, the Home Office Pathologist who had carried out the autopsy, gave it as his opinion that although a blow from such a weapon might have been a contributory cause of death, it would not have killed a man of normal health. Mr Prosper, it appeared, was suffering from an advanced cardiac degeneration, a condition popularly known as fatty degeneration of the heart, probably the result of his life-long sedentary occupation.

'If it hadn't been for Summerson,' said Junior Counsel, as he and Franks walked back from Court, 'he'd have been booked for murder, that's for sure.'

'It was illogical, whichever way you look at it,' said Franks. 'If he meant to kill him, the fact that he didn't hit him hard enough to kill a healthy man, and only happened to kill him because he was unhealthy, shouldn't have reduced the charge from murder to manslaughter.'

'He was lucky,' said Junior Counsel.

'It's not the sort of luck I'd care for myself,' said Franks. 'A hardened criminal might laugh off a five-year sentence. Not Manifold. It'll crucify him.'

They walked on for some distance in silence. Franks said, 'And he's not the only person in trouble.'

This was true. When Sam Collard removed his work to another firm, Mr Goodnight had decided that it was time he retired. He had overlooked the fact that this step invited an automatic inspection of his affairs by the Revenue. He was now faced with criminal charges of tax evasion, the certainty of a crippling fine, and the possibility of imprisonment.

'When you think it through,' said Junior Counsel, 'really the only person who came well out of it was old Prosper. A quick death instead of months of hospital and misery.'

Laurence Meynell

THE WINNING TRICK

Meredith Lawson was often referred to as 'the jolliest man in Midhampton'. Certainly it would seem that he had plenty to be jolly about. He was qualified both as a lawyer and an accountant; and of these two brainy professions had chosen to follow the law.

Everyone in Midhampton agreed that 'Merry L', as he was popularly known, must be making a very comfortable living for himself; one or two of the more thoughtful ones sometimes wondered how in a small country town such a prosperous practice could be built up.

The Midhampton ladies naturally wondered why he had not yet married; when he would marry; and who would be the lucky girl when he did marry. At coffee mornings and over afternoon bridge tables the matter was frequently discussed. Sometimes, ladies being what they are, with a dash of maliciousness to give piquancy to the talk.

'At forty any normal man *ought* to be married,' one sharp-tongued female declared, 'but then, of course, he may not be normal. We see plenty of that sort of thing these days, don't we? If you ask me he's a bit of a mother's boy still – this going off every weekend to see his old mother, it's all very devoted and nice, of course; but, still, at his age, I ask you!'

Echoes of that sort of talk sometimes filtered back to Meredith, but he didn't seem in the least worried by them. He was forty-one; he worked hard; he lived well.

He was in his office by nine o'clock every morning; every midday he lunched rather too lavishly at the Conservative Club; on very rare occasions he might go in the evening up to the links for a mild round of golf; sometimes he took his boat out in the estuary; but nothing very strenuous or serious. 'My recreation is my work,' he was wont to say, but nobody ever thought of him as a dull dog. Very much the reverse. He had a smile and a joke for everybody wherever he went and in these days a man like that is bound to be popular, so it was generally felt that 'Merry L' deserved his nickname and if, on many an evening, he chose to stay on working in his office long after his devoted staff had gone that was his concern and good luck to him.

Meredith Lawson's devoted staff was thirty-five years of age, a completely competent shorthand typist, an absolutely reliable secretary, Mollie Janes. Miss Mollie Janes. No beauty; but, if she took her glasses off for a moment, her face was suddenly seen to have a lot of force and character. She had been born in a village five miles outside Midhampton and had got away from it as soon as she could. Her father and mother were strong Chapel people, and although their daughter never now went to chapel they were under the fond delusion that she had grown up a virtuous, God-fearing woman.

Maybe she was virtuous in a way. Hate is a great virtue, if you hate the right things. Meredith Lawson's thirty-five-year-old secretary had grown up with a passionate hatred of what she thought of as the hypocritical narrowness of Chapel folk and she was contemptuous of their philosophy of contentment. Mollie Janes was not content with her lot and had every intention of improving it. As for being God-fearing, since she didn't know where God was to be found, or what He wanted, she didn't see that there was anything to be afraid of.

Very little of this was realised by the small social

world in Midhampton to which Mollie belonged. Not that she went about a great deal. She lived in a two-roomed flat in Paston Road which was an easy cycle ride from Meredith Lawson's office.

'Why don't you get a car, Mollie?' she was frequently asked. 'A little runabout of some kind.' To which, with her slightly condescending smile, she would invariably reply that she didn't want a runabout, when she got a car it would be a good one. At weekends and on summer evenings she spent a good deal of time at the tennis club. She was not a particularly graceful player, but she was a determined one; and she usually managed to reach the final of any tournament she entered.

In the office she was all that Meredith Lawson could want in the way of a secretary; indeed, truth to tell, she was so efficient that there were times when he was a wee bit scared of her.

Not infrequently he had to remind her that working hours were over. 'Time you were off, Miss Janes.'

'I'll just finish these two letters.'

And when the impeccably typed letters were finished she didn't hurry over the business of covering the electric typewriter and generally tidying up. There was time for Lawson to ask, *'What are you doing this evening, Mollie? Anything special? Why shouldn't we – ?'* but of course he never did, and it was impossible to guess from his secretary's demeanour whether she wanted him to or not.

What was certain was that once Mollie Janes had gone Lawson felt a little easier. He expanded. He unlocked the small compartment beneath his desk and took out the bottle of Grant's whisky which, he fondly imagined, nobody knew about. He made quite certain that the outer office was empty and the door locked. He opened the private safe and drew out Mrs Fanshawe's papers . . . The office was not open on Saturdays.

'No point in working yourself to death,' Lawson said

one evening with his customary laugh, to which Mollie replied, a little dryly, 'I have no intention of doing so.' Then, after a pause, 'I expect you'll be going to see your mother as usual?'

'Yes. The old lady looks forward to seeing me. I can't imagine why.' Another jolly laugh.

'In Bolton, is it, that she lives?'

'Up that way. In that direction. North. A deuce of a long drive. I suppose you'll be playing tennis, will you?'

Yes, Mollie would be playing tennis. 'There's a club match,' she explained, 'and I'm playing for the first team.'

'Good for you. And I'll bet you win.'

They both laughed.

People, even shrewd and calculating people, can easily make false assumptions. Crooked lawyer Meredith Lawson assumed that his secretary would be displaying her tennis powers on the courts of the Midhampton Club. It never occurred to him to enquire where else Mollie might be playing; he had overlooked the fact that occasionally there are such things as away matches.

Anyone heading north from Midhampton naturally leaves the town by the Bardon Road, which is what Lawson did, and the more townspeople who watched him go by and thought 'There's Merry L off to see his old mother again,' the better as far as he was concerned.

He drove a Jag. A long, black, sleek, expensive beauty; a car of which he was extremely fond, many of his friends envious. No little runabout, this.

Six miles along the Bardon Road there is an insignificant turning on the left. The thundering north-bound traffic takes no notice of it; indeed most of the drivers don't know it exists.

But Meredith Lawson knew. He used it every weekend. On this particular Saturday morning he went through his usual cautious procedure.

A quarter of a mile from the turn he slowed the Jag down and concentrated on the rear mirror. A huge eightwheel Scammel passed him and behind it the road was momentarily clear. Not a car in sight, so no Midhampton eyes to worry about. He accelerated, swung the Jag off the Brandon Road and began to hum to himself in happy anticipation.

Mollie Janes' tennis match was against a club Midhampton had never played before – Banley. 'The courts are difficult to find,' the secretary warned everybody, 'they're right in the wilds.'

Mollie was driven there by her partner in the Ladies' Doubles and on the way her thoughts ran, as they often did, on Meredith Lawson and the office. She wondered if Lawson had yet tumbled to the fact that she knew all about the small locked compartment under his desk; she wondered, not for the first time, why, with all the rest of the papers open to her, she was never allowed to see Mrs Fanshawe's . . .

The Banley courts were good, the Banley team was strong; but thanks to stalwart work by Mollie and her partner Midhampton just managed to win. It was after seven when they started for home. On the way there they had twice got lost in a maze of small roads and Mollie's companion was convinced that she knew a better way back.

She was wrong. After ten minutes she had to confess that she had no idea how to get out of the bewildering tangle of lanes in which they were trapped. Not only were the lanes confusing but they appeared to be uninhabited. 'The very first person we see I'll ask,' declared Mollie, who hated indecision of any sort. The first person they saw appeared shortly; he was in uniform and was wearing a peaked cap. He was standing at the entrance to what seemed to be the courtyard of a big house.

Mollie got out of the car and approached him. Now she could see that the 'courtyard' was more like a carpark. There were at least a dozen cars in it, all of the large expensive sort. Was it a smart set country house party, she wondered; or possibly a top executives' weekend conference? All these thoughts were suddenly knocked out of her head. Amongst the cars, straight ahead of her, unmistakeable and undeniable, was Meredith Lawson's Jag. She knew the car and knew its number; there was no possibility of error, it was Lawson's Jag.

The uniformed attendant told her how to get back on to the Midhampton road. She thanked him, and just before turning away asked 'Oh, by the way, what is this nice-looking house?'

'Used to be Banley Manor, Miss. Now it's a private club. Casino.' He gave her a friendly smile. 'But I wouldn't think of trying to join if I were you, Miss; you want a lot of money to play here.'

Lawson swung the Jag into the courtyard of the Manor Club Casino and was greeted by the attendant. Lawson always had a friendly word and a joke for anyone who served him in any way and was popular with servants.

'Good luck, Mr Lawson.'

'Thanks, William. Usual crowd here?'

'Usual lot, sir,' William confirmed. 'Or most of 'em anyway.'

'Then I shall need to be lucky,' Lawson said. Both men laughed.

As Lawson went into the house the old, old feeling that he knew so well, gambler's fever, was already taking possession of him. Saliva was coming into his mouth a little more freely than usual, the palms of his hands were beginning to be moist with sweat. He smiled pleasantly at the exotic beauty in charge of the reception desk and went up to the High Stakes room, his heart thumping.

Inside the High Stakes room he sniffed familiar air. Air into which sunlight and the freshness of the outside were never allowed to intrude. The decoration and furniture were heavily rococo, the curtains of deep red velvet, the chandeliers elaborate. There was no clock to be seen anywhere; time and the outside world were deliberately excluded here; this was the Temple of Chance and its ceremonies and proceedings were conducted with almost religious solemnity. He stood for a moment surveying it all, infinitely glad to have come; the office, Mollie Janes, all the nonsense about a doting old mother somewhere up North forgotten. The addict was now in his element and he was happy . . .

. . . *faites vos jeux* . . . *rien ne va plus* . . . then the click-click-clickety-click of the tantalising little ivory ball; then abruptly no more clicks; a few seconds' silence; the decision of Fate as the croupier called out a number and a sudden release through the overheated room of pent-up excitement and disappointment mixed. Then that bored and totally emotionless voice again, *faites vos jeux, messieurs, mesdames* . . .

Many hours later Lawson placed his last stake; he lost, as he had been doing all evening and he decided to leave.

'Goodnight, Mr Lawson. See you next weekend, I hope.'

Lawson managed a rather poor ghost of his usual cheery smile. 'Yes, I'll be back next weekend,' he promised.

Outside the night air was cold and he was glad of it; he had drunk a lot of whisky and lost a lot of money. But of course bad luck mustn't prevent your doing the right thing. William was still on duty in the carpark and

Lawson handed him a couple of pound notes. William was grateful; he liked Meredith Lawson, a gentleman who always behaved as a gentleman should . . .

Lawson drove the Jag carefully along the now empty roads; he certainly didn't want to be breathalysed on top of such a disastrous evening. He had lost something over three thousand pounds, and that, he had to admit to himself, was a hell of a lot of money, especially coming, as it did, after two other unlucky weekends. It wouldn't mean much, he reflected bitterly, to the dark gentleman sitting next to him in the High Stakes room who looked as though he had a couple of oil wells in his pocket and who was putting twice that amount on a single spin of the roulette wheel; but for him, Meredith Lawson, three thousand was a hell of a lot of money. He ran his tongue over dry lips when he thought of it . . . *Well*, he told himself, *I can't go on being so unlucky. Luck's got to turn some time. I'll be there next weekend and win it all back*, and meanwhile, he thought, meanwhile thank God for trusting old ladies like Lucy Fanshawe who as long as they get their dividends paid regularly haven't the ghost of a notion of what's happening to their capital . . .

On Monday morning in the office Mollie Janes asked: 'How were things up North with your mother, Mr Lawson? Did you have a good trip?'

'It's a long way,' Lawson answered. 'Tiring. But the old lady is in good shape, I'm glad to say, though she doesn't get any younger, of course.'

Which of us does, thought thirty-five-year-old Mollie Janes, we none of us get any younger, and maybe it's time to do something about it . . .

'And how did your tennis go?' Lawson asked.

His secretary smiled happily at him. 'Oh, I thoroughly enjoyed my day,' she told him. 'I won.'

Lawson nodded. I'm sure you did, he thought a trifle

sourly. Well, someone has got to win sometimes, I suppose . . .

On Friday of that week the secretary of the Midhampton tennis club was dismayed to be told that Mollie Janes would not be available for the weekend match. 'Oh dear,' she protested, 'it's such an important match and we were relying on you.'

Mollie shook her head. 'Sorry,' she said, 'I shall be busy.'

The unhappy secretary wanted to ask *if you aren't going to play in the match what on earth will you be doing*? but she didn't quite like to. Not with Mollie Janes. Mollie Janes was not the sort of person who encouraged questions like that.

On Saturday morning Mollie had her usual leisurely breakfast – a cup of coffee and *The Daily Telegraph* crossword – and then packed a picnic lunch and strapped it on to the carrier of her cycle. She didn't mind meagre midday fare as she was hoping to do better in the evening.

Just before seven she appeared at the entrance to the courtyard of Banley Manor. Her first quick glance told her that she was right. The Jag was there.

William recognized her and wondered if she had lost her way again. But Mollie didn't ask the way. She asked, 'Is Mr Lawson here?'

'Yes, Miss. Mr Lawson's in the Club.'

'I'm his secretary and I have an urgent message for him.'

'You had better see the young lady at the desk inside, Miss. She'll put you right.'

The young lady at the desk inside looked a little doubtful. 'If it's important,' she said hesitantly.

'It is,' Mollie assured her. 'Very important.'

'You'll have to see Luigi, then. In the room on the right at the top of the staircase. Ask for Luigi. He's in charge there.'

Mollie went up the fine staircase and cautiously opened the big door on the right-hand side.

The first thing she was aware of was an almost palpable silence punctuated by a curious clicking noise.

Then the clicking suddenly stopped and a couple of seconds afterwards a voice droned out '*Huit, noir, pair, manque, première* . . . and a general buzz of chattering voices broke out.

Meredith Lawson had been watching the wayward little white ball as intently as anyone. He had put the stake which he couldn't afford on what he always thought of as his lucky number, 18. 8 was no good to him. Luck was going against him as badly as it had done on the previous week.

'Christ,' he muttered, 'this is disastrous.'

He raised his eyes and looked across the room. He didn't believe what he saw. Mollie Janes, his secretary, was standing just inside the door and Luigi was approaching her, presumably to find out who she was and what she wanted.

Lawson swore blasphemously again under his breath. He couldn't make head or tail of this for the moment; but it had to be dangerous. Highly dangerous. He had always been a bit suspicious of the Janes woman, had always suspected that there were deep waters there.

He moved quickly across the room and reached her just before Luigi did. Mollie studied his appearance. He looked white and unhappy. He looked to her like a gambler who had been losing a lot of money and who was alarmed at being found out.

'What in the name of God are you doing here?' Lawson asked.

'I was just wondering how your old mother was this weekend,' Mollie answered with a smile which Lawson didn't for one second regard as friendly. *She knows something*, he thought, *but how much? She's dangerous*. He realised that he must make an effort to salvage something; it might be possible to get together some sort of protective camouflage . . .

He steadied his voice with an effort. 'I think perhaps I had better explain things a little,' he said.

His secretary smiled at him again. 'Good idea,' she agreed. 'Why don't we have dinner somewhere? I had a very inadequate lunch.'

Halfway between Banley Manor and Midhampton there was an expensive country restaurant, The Baron of Beef. In the overheated, over-comfortable grill room Lawson ate very little and drank a lot. Mollie both ate and drank well: she was enjoying herself.

The lawyer was trying to get his defences together: he remembered the wise old maxim *Say nothing, give nothing away*; but after the first course, eaten almost entirely in a strained silence, he could contain himself no longer.

'How did you know where I was? What on earth made you go there?'

'I saw the Jag in the courtyard and wondered how you were getting on.'

Liar, Lawson thought. Aloud he said, as offhandedly as he could manage, 'I go there occasionally, just to have a bit of a gamble.'

Mollie nodded. 'I've never played roulette,' she said. 'It must be fun – especially with somebody else's money.'

'What on earth do you mean by that?' The words did their best to sound virtuously indignant but they were unconvincing: the face was white and frightened.

It had been something of a long shot and it had gone home. She was sure now. Now suspicions she had entertained for a long time hardened into certainty. 'I'll bet Mrs Fanshawe doesn't know all that happens to her money,' she said.

There was a long silence during which Meredith Lawson weighed up the pros and cons. He added everything up, balanced possibilities against certainties and then raised his glass and took a mouthful of wine as a silent toast to a decision he had just come to – this woman was too dangerous to him and he would have to kill her.

'Presumably you have been doing some private detective work?' he asked.

'Just a little. Enough. One isn't a fool, you know.'

'No.' (With a ghost of a smile.) 'I never thought you were. You're much too clever to be thought a fool,' (but not clever enough to escape the results of your folly, he thought). 'So what do you propose to do about it all?'

'It's rather what *you* propose to do about it, Meredith.' (She had never used his Christian name before.) 'There *is* a nice, comfortable way out of everything for both of us, of course.'

'There is?'

'Certainly.' A long pause, then: 'We can get married and keep it all in the family.'

The little social world of Midhampton fairly buzzed with news of the engagement. The coffee mornings and the bridge tables hummed with it.

'Not such a mother's boy after all then,' and, 'She's done pretty well for herself,' represented the general view with, 'Do you suppose she'll make him take up tennis?' as a semi-facetious afterthought.

What about the wedding? All the Midhampton ladies wanted to know, since for some curious psychological reason any wedding, of anybody, anywhere, has a compelling fascination for all women.

'She'll want to make a splash of it,' was the consensus of opinion, a consensus which was entirely accurate. Having waited until she was thirty-five and then having brought off a coup which seemed to her to be entirely satisfactory Mollie Janes had no intention of being fobbed off with a hole and corner affair in a registry office.

She wanted St Martin's Parish Church (into which building she had been only twice in her life). The vicar, or better still the Bishop, if Meredith could pull any strings). Herself in flowing white. The organ pealing and the choir belting out her choice of hymns. *The Midhampton News* alerted so that photographers and reporters would be there in plenty. In other words, the lot. All of which was anathema to Meredith Lawson; but this was a fact that nobody could possibly guess from his behaviour.

Over the dinner table at the Baron of Beef he had come to the only decision which seemed to him possible, and now his every act had to be directed to achieving that highly desirable end with the minimum of risk to himself. So to all outward seeming he became the very model of the doting husband-to-be. Everything that Mollie proposed about the wedding he concurred in, apparently enthusiastically.

The ladies of Midhampton were amused to see how completely devoted he had become. 'Meredith Lawson has got it badly,' they told one another. 'Lucky girl.'

Together with Mollie he gloated over the wedding presents while secretly wondering how on earth people could spend money on such objects.

The tennis club sent six glass tumblers and Lawson, who had started to drink more heavily than usual, had to allow a certain amount of sense in that. Mrs Fanshawe sent a piece of Chelsea china, a piece she didn't really want to part with but it came, 'With my best wishes and gratitude for the close attention you have always given to my affairs'.

'Don't you think that kind of her?' Mollie asked.

'Very.'

'In the circumstances,' Mollie went on, 'I'd say it was very kind indeed.' She laughed. She had Lawson in a corner from which he couldn't escape. He knew it and she knew he knew it. She found the situation amusing. She also found it exciting. The do-your-duty-and-be-satisfied-with-your-lot-it-will-all-be-made-up-to-you-in-the-next-world attitude of her parents had bred violent reaction in Mollie Janes. It was something she rejected utterly. Merely remembering it made her furiously angry. To get everything she could out of life, just like everybody else was doing, was her philosophy; and now she was delighted at how well she was beginning to succeed in it.

That Meredith Lawson was dishonest didn't worry her in the slightest. Honest, dishonest, she dismissed the words. The terms she understood were successful, and unsuccessful; money and no money. Lawson had got his hands on a lot of money: she had got her hands on him and they were going to enjoy life together.

In the office there was no point in keeping the contents of the private safe secret. Mollie gave a little gasp as much of admiration as of surprise when she saw what had happened to Mrs Fanshawe's money.

'My God, you have soaked the old lady!' she exclaimed.

'I send her a cheque for what she thinks is her dividend every half-year,' Lawson said, 'so what's she got to grumble about?'

'And you will be able to go on doing that?'

'Of course,' Lawson lied. 'I was at Banley Manor last weekend. My luck's turned.'

'It must be because we're going to be married,' Mollie said. 'It's going to be lucky for both of us.'

Lawson smiled.

She didn't try to stop him gambling. In a way she approved of it; it fitted in with her philosophy of life; if you won it was money, lovely money, for nothing. If you lost, pick yourself up and have another go. Lawson, for his part, lost no opportunity of showing Midhampton how much he was looking forward to his marriage and how happy he was in the company of his amorata.

He allowed her to show him off at the tennis club on a couple of occasions, and was secretly a little disconcerted to note the energetic way in which she ran about the court.

'I suppose you're good at all sports,' he suggested over tea in the club house. 'Unlike me, I'm afraid: the only thing I was ever any use at was swimming.'

'That's one thing I could never manage,' answered Mollie, still hot and flushed after her success on the court. 'I can hardly swim at all.'

'What a shame,' her fiancé said, and he managed to sound as though he meant it. Midhampton boasted one eating establishment in the luxury class – La Ronde – and Mollie made it plain that she would like to be taken there as often as possible. It was an excellent place to show off her capture; and, as far as Lawson was concerned, it was an equally excellent place in which to demonstrate how happy he was to be captured.

Over dinner she would talk endlessly about the impending wedding ceremony, discussing every detail, changing her mind, suggesting alterations, worrying about the bridesmaids' dresses, the choir, the hymn tunes, and God knows what.

Astute woman though she was in many ways she utterly failed to realise the murderous boredom with which Lawson listened to this farrago. He was too clever for her. He let her have her head which anyway was easy for him because he didn't give a tuppenny damn what the bridesmaids wore or what the choir was to sing; what he was interested in was the honeymoon.

But he played his cards very carefully. Softee, softee catchee monkey. 'In the autumn,' he said, 'we can have a really good honeymoon. There's a legal convention in New York I've been invited to. We can take wives. So we shall have a week in New York, where they are sure to do us well and then, when the convention's over, you and I can go over to California and have a fortnight or so there – how's that?'

Mollie's eyes glistened. She said it sounded absolutely marvellous. 'Clever you,' she said.

'But it's not till the autumn,' Lawson went on, 'and we must have some sort of token honeymoon to go on with. What about a few days on the boat?'

'Oh, that old boat of yours!'

'Well, I shall enjoy it and I think you would too.'

Mollie laughed. 'Oh, all right,' she said, 'as long as you take me to America in the autumn.'

'Merry L' was seemingly never merrier than in the weeks before the wedding. He told anyone who cared to listen all about the honeymoon plans, three days on the boat first of all; then a week in London doing a theatre every night and hitting the high spots generally, and last of all New York and California – 'that must wait till the autumn,' he explained, 'but isn't it something marvellous for us to look forward to?'

The bridge tables and the coffee morning discussed it all frequently and in detail. The general verdict lay, as feminine verdicts tend to, halfway between admiration and envy. *She's played her cards pretty well, I always said she was a bit of a deep one*, was what Midhampton thought about it. On the morning of the great day Mollie Janes listened anxiously to the weather forecast. The gods, in whom she did not normally believe, were quite capable, she felt sure, of spoiling everything by providing twenty-four hours of pouring rain; but, no, the weather man was quite chirpy and cheerful for once – plenty of sunshine and a strong southerly wind which would keep the rain away.

Lawson listened just as anxiously to the same broadcast. He didn't care about the sunshine: what interested him was the strong southerly wind. A strong southerly wind was exactly what he wanted. It meant they would be meeting a heavy swell as soon as they rounded the point of the estuary and turned into Wilmer Sound.

St Martin's church was crowded for the wedding. In one way or another Lawson seemed to know nearly everybody in the town, and if Mollie didn't have many real friends at least the tennis club turned up in force to support her. She was a woman who made plans to meet all contingencies and liked to see those plans succeeding. All her carefully thought out, detailed arrangements for the ceremony went just as she wanted them to. The organ pealed, the choir sang, the vicar droned, the cameras clicked, the reporters scribbled, the bridesmaids looked sweet. Somewhere in the middle of it all the archaic words were pronounced. The sun shone, the rain clouds were chased away by the southerly wind. It was all highly satisfactory.

So too was the reception where the cake was cut; the telegrams were read out; the champagne was poured; and the best man cracked the inevitable jokes. Finally it was over. *Christ Almighty*, Lawson thought as he was changing into more workaday clothes, *all that flapdoodle has cost a pretty penny*! but this wasn't what he said to Mollie. What he said to her was, 'Now for the real fun of the day, just the two of us together.'

Mollie, who had been given a free hand in all the wedding arrangements, had wisely been content to let Lawson plan the first days of honeymoon. It wasn't what she would have chosen for herself but, after all, there was an extravagant week in London and then, later, New York and California to look forward to.

'We'll go to Banley Manor for a couple of hours,' he said, 'just to try our luck. Then the Baron of Beef for a real slap-up dinner. Then the boat, just the two of us alone.'

'Marvellous,' Mollie said.

Naturally the two hours at the casino stretched to

nearly double that time. Mollie, who had never before played roulette, won consistently; the obvious jokes about 'virgin luck' were made, but they didn't trouble Mollie who was just over a hundred pounds to the good when they decided to leave.

Even Lawson had ended up on the right side for once; he was at pains to have a carefully chosen word with Luigi as they were leaving. 'You'll get a new customer now, Luigi. We'll both be here as soon as we can.'

And in the courtyard it was 'Good night, sir. Good night, madam,' from William, and from Lawson a cheery 'Good night, William. You'll be seeing a good deal of us both in the future.'

In the Baron of Beef Mollie listened to Lawson ordering the wine, and half protested that after all the champagne at the reception she didn't really want anything else: 'If I have much more I shall go straight off to sleep – and that wouldn't please you at all, would it, Meredith?'

The archness underlying the words sent a shudder down Lawson's spine. He had never in his life desired intimate physical contact with any woman; the thought of it with this particular one, his own private secretary who had spied on him and who fondly imagined she could destroy him if she wanted to, revolted him.

None of which, of course, showed in his face as he smilingly replied that one's wedding night was a bit of a special occasion after all, and just a glass wouldn't hurt, anyway.

On the wall there was a poster advertising a Gala Dinner with a cabaret in three weeks' time.

'It would be rather fun to go to that, don't you think?' Lawson said. 'I'll book a table.'

When they finally got to the jetty where the boat was moored everything was quiet and deserted. Lawson ran the Jag into the otherwise empty carpark and said, now with genuine feeling in his voice, 'How marvellous. Just the two of us, alone.'

The moon was shining, but some whisps of cloud were scudding across it. Mollie glanced up a little apprehensively and asked: 'Is it going to be rough?' Lawson laughed reassuringly. 'Good Lord, no. Just a puff of wind now and again. Nothing to worry about.'

Going quietly along the estuary it wasn't rough. Mollie sat on the tiny deck with her back to the low rail; she was glad of the cold night air after the stuffy atmosphere she had been in most of the day. The rhythmic *chug, chug, chug* of the engine was soporific. She closed her eyes. 'I told you I would go to sleep,' she said. She was more than content to leave everything to Lawson who evidently knew exactly what he was doing. Occasionally he would call her attention to something.

'See that flashing red light – on, then eight seconds darkness, then on again – that's Wilmer Point; just beyond it we get into the Sound.'

'How far are we going?'

'Not much further. I know a little creek at the head of the Sound where we can tie up comfortably and then we'll go below and turn in.'

'I must say you've got it worked out marvellously, Meredith.'

Lawson laughed. 'I hope so. You're not cold, are you?'

'It is getting a shade chilly.'

'Everything prepared for,' Lawson said. From somewhere beneath his legs he produced a Thermos flask.

'Lovely hot coffee,' he said. 'Pour yourself out a cup.'

The coffee was undoubtedly of good quality; it was splendidly hot; it was also heavily laced with a sedative.

'Delicious,' Mollie said. 'I had no idea being on a boat could be such fun.'

By the time they rounded the point and got into the Sound she was asleep, so that she was blissfully unaware of the alteration in the boat's movement as it met the suddenly lumpy, choppy water.

When he was well out in the middle of the Sound where the water was deepest and the notoriously awkward cross currents ran Lawson quietly rose from where he was sitting and crossed the few feet to where his secretary-wife sprawled back against the low rail. She was fast asleep.

You bitch, he thought, *I'll teach you not to interfere in my affairs.*

He put both his hands under the bend of her knees and bracing himself for the effort with a sudden heave sent her backwards over the rail into the sea.

A single scream and that was all. Then there was silence, only the thump of the choppy water against the boat and the slight persistent singing of the wind.

Mollie Janes, the ambitious secretary who had found out too much, who was a very poor swimmer anyway and who on that particular occasion was in no condition to swim at all, was drowned in the treacherous waters of Wilmer Sound.

Meredith Lawson cruised round for a while, being in no hurry to get back. He could give what timetable he liked of the night's events and no one could contradict him.

Naturally Midhampton fairly buzzed with news of the tragedy. The local paper went to town about it; the bridge tables and the coffee mornings talked about little else.

Everybody heard, and repeated to everybody else, how Lawson had cruised up and down Wilmer Sound desperately searching for any sign of his bride and how he had finally brought his boat back to the jetty and gone to the police station in a distraught state.

What could be done then was done, but it was very little and all to no avail. Lawson told his boating friends how it had happened. 'The engine was spluttering a little and I was bent double trying to spot what was wrong when suddenly *wham* one of those freak Wilmer waves hit us and knocked me off my balance. I heard a shriek and, God dammit, that's all there was to it; Mollie had gone.'

His boating friends needed no convincing. They knew the hazards of Wilmer Sound very well. They nodded in wise agreement. 'You can get those freak waves any time of day or night in Wilmer Sound,' they said.

The tennis club would see Mollie Lawson (*née* Janes) no more. It was all very sad and everyone felt that the news headline 'Honeymoon Tragedy' was only too well justified.

Meredith Lawson was faced with the problem of finding a new secretary; he let it be known that he was going to take his time about doing it and everybody agreed that this was wise.

In a kindly way many people wondered how the poor man would manage.

Mrs Fanshawe, who when her husband died had been left a rich widow, wondered. A few days after the tragedy she invited Lawson to have tea with her so that she could commiserate with him.

In the middle of tea Bessie, the maid, announced that a Mr Wright was at the door.

'Mr Wright?'

'Of Wright and Pringle, he says, madam.'

Mrs Fanshawe knew the firm Wright and Pringle by name. Lawyers, but not her lawyers. She was puzzled.

'And he's got a policeman with him,' the maid blandly added.

'A *policeman?*' Mrs Fanshawe was alarmed, she glanced for guidance at Lawson who was beginning to be even more alarmed than she was and was doing his best not to show it.

'Well, I suppose you had better tell Mr Wright to come in,' Mrs Fanshawe said, 'and the policeman.'

If Mr Wright, of Wright and Pringle, was embarrassed at finding Meredith Lawson in the room he gave no indication of the fact. He was admirably concise and direct in what he had to say.

He told Mrs Fanshawe that he represented the late Mrs Lawson or, as he knew her, Miss Mollie Janes; that although she had worked for some years as secretary to another and well-known solicitor in the town (he bowed slightly towards Lawson) she had always preferred to have her own small legal matters dealt with by Wright and Pringle.

'No doubt she was entitled to do that if she so chose,' Mrs Fanshawe said, 'but how does that concern me?' and Meredith Lawson, sitting silent, fighting hard not to betray anything of the fear he was beginning to feel, wondered desperately how it was going to concern him . . .

'Shortly before her marriage,' Mr Wright continued, 'Miss Mollie Janes, as she then was, left a sealed envelope in my care with instructions that in the event of any unexpected accident happening to her I was to open it and act on its contents.'

'What an odd thing to do!' Mrs Fanshawe exclaimed. 'Don't you think it odd, Mr Lawson?'

Meredith Lawson had by this time gone white in the face, but he somehow managed a wry smile. 'She was always a very practical person,' he said.

'And what were the contents of the sealed envelope?' Mrs Fanshawe asked.

Mr Wright held a paper in his hand and he was careful not to let go of it.

'My late client's instructions are,' he said, 'that in the event of any unexpected accident happening to her I was to seek the cooperation of the police, and together we were to advise you, Mrs Fanshawe, to look into the matter of your investments.'

'My investments!' Mrs Fanshawe exclaimed. 'But that is ridiculous. Mr Lawson here has always handled all that business for me. He pays me my cheques regularly.'

'In that case, madam,' the policeman said, 'there is obviously nothing to worry about. We will just go through the formality of asking Mr Lawson to let us look at the books and no doubt everything will be in order. Are you happy about that, Mr Lawson?'

Meredith Lawson didn't answer immediately. He was thinking, running a sequence of things through his mind like the shots in a film. The whole silly affair seemed so short, looking back on it. A brilliant start, no one could deny him that, he had snapped up good business all round, people trusted him; Mrs Fanshawe, richly widowed, had trusted him; then the first, almost accidental, visit to Banley Manor, a lucky visit so of course he had gone again; then he went on going; the bug hit him; the fever seized him; he had become a gambler and he had to go on gambling; so the money had to come from somewhere; it was all going to be paid back in time of course. And now there wasn't time. Time had run out . . .

'Are you happy about that, Mr Lawson?' the policeman repeated.

By this time every vestige of colour had drained from Meredith Lawson's face and he couldn't manage even the ghost of a smile.

'Not exactly happy,' he made answer, rising from his seat, 'but let's go and get it over.'

Anne Morice

A GOOD NIGHT'S SLEEP

Anthony Morrison was awakened at three in the morning by Angie's snores and, for not less than the fiftieth time since their marriage, wished that one of them were dead. The only exceptional part of it was that the wish was now about to be granted.

Unaware of this, he gave himself up to meditating on his grievances, of which the chief one was that it should be three a.m. and neither earlier nor later. Between one and two o'clock the links with dreams and drowsiness were often strong enough to pull him back into them, and sometimes that second sleep was more protective and cocoon-like than the first. Four o'clock was more bearable too, in its different way, specially in summer when the first light was breaking and the nameless fears and apprehensions of the night were beginning to recede. Then he could tell himself in a sensible, tolerant way that five hours' sleep at a stretch wasn't all that bad for a man in his sixties; and also how lucky he was, in most other ways, to be married to such a pretty young wife. Well, comparatively young, at any rate; and successful too, in her way, no question about it. That television soap opera had been running for seven years now. He knew this for a fact because towards the end of her life it had been one of the few programmes which Peggy, his first wife, enjoyed watching. Nowadays it often amused him to remember how, although they had never met, Peg had come to feel that she knew Angie, the real Angie and not just the character she played, as well as one of her own sisters.

Four o'clock was better still on a day when she was going to be working, because then it would be almost time for him to get up anyway; to make the toast and coffee, lightly boil the eggs and bring it all upstairs on a tray, then shake Angie awake and warn her that the studio car would be due in an hour's time. And always at the back of his mind, as he went about these tasks, he would cherish the prospect, like a child hugging a treat in store, of having the whole day to himself, and he would make jolly plans to take Nanki-Pooh for a walk on the beach and have a glass of wine with his lunch, to relax him for that lovely quiet siesta afterwards.

No such consolations were the slightest use to him at three o'clock, as the snores, continuous, although varying in volume and pitch, went relentlessly on.

He turned first on one side, then on the other, buried his head under the pillow, withdrew it again as suffocation became imminent and finally, after twenty minutes of this torture, sat up and groped for his dressing gown pocket and the secret supply of ear plugs. They were neither comfortable, nor very effective, but in the last resort had been known to save his sanity.

The movement must have roused Angie from the profoundest depths of sleep, for she turned from her back on to her side and miraculously the noise ceased. He could just see the outline of her head, which looked as big as a birdcage, signifying that she had her rollers in and therefore, thank God for that, tomorrow was a working day.

Still sitting up, with both arms stretched forward over the eiderdown, he waited, rigid and tense, until he had counted to fifty. Still the blessed silence continued and he gently lowered himself back on the pillow, closed his eyes and instantly fell asleep.

*

125

Two feet away, Angela Morrison lay on her side with her eyes wide open, watching in near despair for some light to appear in the narrow gap in the curtains. She had not looked at her illuminated clock, for she could judge to within minutes what time it was. Waking between three and half past was becoming a regular habit now and there were really only two remedies available to her. One was to take a sleeping pill and the other to switch on the light and read a book for twenty minutes. Neither could be put into practice, however, since the first would be disastrous on a morning when she had to be made up and on the set by nine o'clock, and the second would inevitably awaken Tony.

He would be understanding and sympathetic, beg her to go ahead and promise her faithfully that it wouldn't disturb him in the least, but she knew only too well that the tension set up by his silent martyrdom would not only destroy her concentration, making the printed word meaningless, but would effectively banish sleep as well.

So she lay as still as she could, going over and over her lines until they too became meaningless, and thinking what a ravaged old hag would be facing the cameras in the morning.

'Won't do,' she told herself sternly. 'Self discipline, that's what. Compose yourself! Cross ankles, cross wrists, let the blood flow round . . . that's better. Now, at least you can rest and relax, which is better than nothing . . . rest . . . relax . . .'

She was jerked back into full consciousness again by a heaving movement beside her. Tony turned over in his sleep and two seconds later his mouth fell open and the first snore reverberated through the silent bedroom, with the impact of the opening bars of a Wagner overture on a hushed auditorium.

*

It was a relief to find her already up and seated at her dressing table, with most of the rollers scattered all over it, when he brought the breakfast tray in. He thought she looked wretchedly tired and pale, but he knew better by now than to say so and, in any case, the way he was feeling, he probably looked a damn sight worse himself.

'What would you like me to get for dinner?' he asked, pouring out her coffee.

'Nothing, thank you, darling.'

'Oh, why not? I'm sure we'll both need something; and, in case you're relying on the cold beef, I'd better tell you that I used it all up in the rissoles yesterday.'

'I wasn't relying on the cold beef. We're dining out tonight.'

'Are we? Who with?'

'The Arkwrights. Really, darling, your memory!'

'Oh yes, so we are, I do remember now. Sorry! Not very bright at this hour of the morning.'

'Who is?' she asked, going to work with the nail varnish.

'Is anything the matter with that egg?'

'No, it's lovely. Why?'

'You're not eating it.'

'Give me time! I'm not all that hungry, as a matter of fact.'

'All the same, you ought to try and eat something. You've got a long day ahead of you.'

'Don't I know it!'

'Will it be a party tonight, or just us?'

'Just us, I imagine. Jane said not to dress up.'

'That's good!'

'Is it? Sounds a bit boring to me.'

'I hate dressing up, and also it means that it probably won't have to drag on too late. I think we could both do with an early night. That is, I'm sure you could.'

'Do I look ghastly?' she asked, grimacing at her reflection in the mirror.

'Of course you don't, darling. You know I didn't mean that. You look marvellous.'

'Honestly, Tony?'

'Truly and honestly. All I meant was that you've had a terribly tough week, working every day and getting back so late.'

'With a stiff drink and a hot bath waiting for me, and dinner all ready to eat the moment I want it? I'm not really complaining, but I do know what you mean and I'm thankful this is the last day. I just can't wait to laze about on the beach, doing absolutely nothing while you wear yourself out throwing stones for Nanki. Thank God for Friday, is what I say!'

'How about next week? Heavy schedule?'

'Not so bad. If all goes without a hitch today, touch wood, I'll be able to have Monday and Tuesday off.'

'Oh, splendid!' he said fulsomely, stacking mugs and plates on to the tray. 'Four whole days to laze about in! It'll do you all the good in the world.'

Angie flopped herself down and then, as though surrendering to an overpowering impulse, swung her legs up and stretched out full length on the large though chaste-looking bed, and closed her eyes.

'Yes, you really are tired, aren't you?' Jane Arkwright said, coming back from the bathroom. 'I noticed it at dinner.'

'Did I look awful?' Angie asked, still with her eyes closed.

'No, not awful at all, you couldn't if you tried. More like a child who's been kept up too late. I was waiting for you to slide off your chair and fall fast asleep on the floor.'

'No danger of that, the dinner was much too good. Sorry if I wasn't pulling my weight, but it's been one of those weeks and I feel exhausted, to be honest with you.'

'Of course you do, so would anyone. You take on far too much, you know that, don't you? Working under those grisly lights all day and looking after that lay-about husband when you get home at night.'

'Oh, that's not fair, Jane, really it's not. Tony's an angel and awfully good about doing his share, I promise you. He takes care of all the shopping and brings me breakfast in bed; and very often cooks the dinner too. Of course he can't cope with the big chores, like turning out rooms and cleaning the silver and all that. I wouldn't expect him to and I wouldn't want it.'

'So you do the really heavy jobs yourself? Why? I mean, why not get someone in for a few hours twice a week? You must be able to afford that?'

'Yes, I can, and in fact I've tried it once or twice, but it never worked.'

'Tony managed to upset them, I suppose?'

'Not his fault; but he does have terribly high stand-ards and he's awfully meticulous about everything being just so, if you know what I mean? Must be his army training, I think; but he admitted to me that he was much happier managing on his own. Besides, women of that type probably aren't accustomed to taking orders from men.'

'Only women of your type?'

'No, you're being unfair, Jane. I don't mind a bit of scrubbing and polishing now and again. Quite good therapy, actually. It's not that which makes me so tired.'

'What then?'

'Insomnia, I suppose you could call it. I know this sounds disloyal, but you've caught me in a weak moment. I'm getting to breaking point and it's such a relief to talk to somebody . . . what really gets me down is having to share a bed with him. He . . . well . . . he's restless, and it keeps me awake.'

'Snores, you mean?'

'Yes, I'm afraid I do, and the awful thing is that it's getting worse. This'll probably sound melodramatic, but sometimes I feel that it's literally killing me. I haven't had a decent night's sleep for months, except when I take one of my pills, which he doesn't really approve of; and anyway that's out, when I have to work the next day.'

'Surely, the answer is to have separate rooms?'

Angie sighed: 'You make it sound so simple, but it's not, and it wouldn't be the answer at all. I wouldn't dare even to suggest such a thing.'

'Why not, for God's sake?'

'He'd never understand in a million years and he'd be mortally offended. People can never believe they snore, can they? He'd be bound to think it was just an excuse and that I had some quite different reason for wanting a room of my own.'

'You're too soft, Angie, that's your trouble.'

'No, I'm not, it's just that you don't understand how sensitive he is and how important that kind of thing is to him. He's quite a bit older than us, you know, and habits become so deeply ingrained at his age.'

'All the same, they can still be broken.'

'Not this one. At least, I couldn't be the one to break it. It's sort of symbolic, in a way, and he'd think something had gone really wrong with our marriage if I asked for separate bedrooms. He always shared a double bed with his first wife, you know, until she became so ill. I was rather dreading that bit, to be truthful. Not that she died at home, poor thing . . . but . . . well, you know what I mean? But Tony was so thoughtful and understanding about it. He got rid of the old bed and bought a magnificent brand new one. Much more expensive than he could really afford.'

'Although I daresay he doesn't have to fork out for very much else these days,' Jane remarked, turning round and starting to comb her hair.

'Of course, it's different for you and Bob,' Angie said, as though she hadn't heard. 'You two have always had separate rooms.'

'No, not always.'

'Different for you . . . you realise that . . . ' Angie continued in a droning voice. 'You're lucky . . . do you know how lucky . . . ?'

The words trailed off into a mumble, then ceased altogether. There were two seconds of utter silence, followed by a piercing nasal snort, which woke her up and caused Jane to spin round on her dressing table stool.

As though tugged by invisible wires, Angie sat up straight, took a powder compact out of her bag and dabbed at her nose and chin.

'God, I almost did drop off just then,' she remarked in a rueful, humorous tone.

Watching her, Jane said: 'Shall I give you a word of advice, or are you too sleepy to take it in?'

'No, no, wide awake now.'

'All right, then, here's a tip which I can recommend from personal experience. It shouldn't give you any trouble at all, you being a pro. And when I've told you, we'd better buck up and go downstairs, otherwise the boys will be wondering what's become of us.'

As it happened, though, the boys were not wondering anything of the kind, having been engaged in a most frank and interesting discussion of their own.

Tony and Angie lay side by side in the dark, each silently going over the evening with the Arkwrights: in particular, those intimate conversations which had taken place immediately after dinner and, in Angie's case, with a growing sense of desperation.

'Easy as falling off a log for a pro,' Jane had concluded by saying, and indeed it had sounded as though it would be, so why the hell, when it came to the point, was she finding it so hard to get started? What ridiculous inhibition was putting the brake on like this and keeping her silent? And the worst of it was that, in spite of it, she was actually beginning to feel drowsy, simply couldn't make the effort. That hot cocoa Tony had brought upstairs after she was in bed was certainly having an effect. It had been rather filthy too, much stronger and sweeter than she liked, but she had drunk it all down because it was so lovely of him to take all that trouble at the end of a long evening, and he had looked so pleased and proud of himself, dear old darling . . . Oh, come on, now, snap out of it! . . . No good putting it off till you wake up in the small hours. Jane had warned her about that. He might be dead asleep by then and it wouldn't make any impression at all. Got to start as soon as I put the light out and keep it up for as long as I can . . . What's so difficult about that? I, of all people, ought to know what a snore sounds like and how to reproduce it. Perhaps I'm going about it the wrong way . . . might be better to try starting very quietly . . . gradually build up to . . . cres . . . crescendo . . . right, here we go then . . .'

She opened her mouth to draw in a deep breath, then held it for almost a minute, because Tony had turned over and she knew by the slow, rhythmical sounds coming from his side of the bed that she had already left it too late.

Tears of frustration and self-pity almost blinded her and her mind was in utter confusion, as she stretched out a hand and fumbled around on the bedside table for the little bottle. It was not in its usual place, so far away as to be almost out of reach. Was that a message to herself, warning her that she had already taken one? No, couldn't be, she'd have remembered for sure, and she had no recollection of it whatever. Hold on a minute, though! What she did remember, in a blurred sort of way, as though it had happened many years ago, was Tony standing at the foot of the bed and asking her some question and then her own voice replying: 'No, darling, shan't need it tonight'; so that was all right, and better take two, just to be on the safe side . . .

She fell into an uneasy sleep, unaware that she had been repeating the words aloud in a muttered groan: 'be on the safe side . . . safe side . . .'

As usual, Tony was the first out of bed the next morning, though not so early on this occasion, because it was Saturday and Angie was not on call. There was no special breakfast routine at weekends and they ate it when they felt like it. The only strict rule was that she was not to be woken unless the place was actually on fire.

So he stayed comfortably tucked up for as long as he dared, savouring the blissful peace and solitude and occasionally looking out at the unfamiliar view from his dressing room window, and soon after eight he got up and made the bed, carefully flattening and patting the fitted counterpane into place before going into the bathroom.

He was not yet sure how he would cope with the business of changing the sheets when this became necessary, and always provided that the plan continued to work, but he thought there was bound to be one of those launderette places somewhere in the town and one of the girls in the supermarket could probably tell him where it was and how to work the machines. Unfortunately, he had forgotten to ask Bob how he had dealt with that problem, or perhaps he had asked him and had forgotten the answer. There had been quite a lot of wine flowing, one way and another, and the only part of the conversation which still remained vivid in his memory began with Bob saying:

'You've got to strike early, old boy. No good hanging on till three in the morning, when the will power's at its lowest ebb. Just wait till she's out for the count and then make a dash for it. Believe me, I know what I'm talking about.'

'But supposing she were to wake up and find I wasn't there and come looking for me? I'd have to pretend I was feeling ill or something. She'd see through that in a minute and then the fat wouldn't half be in the fire. I know Angie and she'd be off her head with worry.'

'Oh, I daresay, but that's not likely to happen, is it? Not if she'd taken her pills, that is. If she did wake up at some point, chances are she'd think you'd gone to the bathroom and turn over and go to sleep again. Of course, you could only get away with it when you were sure she'd taken her dose, but that's all that concerns you, isn't it? Other days you can make up the lost ground by having a good zizz after lunch.'

Well, he had made absolutely sure. When Angie told him she wouldn't take her pills if he was going to make her a lovely hot drink, he'd waited till she was out of the room, then pinched a couple from the bottle on her bedside table and taken them downstairs with him.

Actually, when he got to the kitchen, he found he was clutching three of the things and he also found that he couldn't remember how many she usually took. More than one, he was pretty certain of that, and once she'd confessed that her head felt so thick and muzzy that she was afraid she must have made a stupid mistake and taken them twice over. That was when they had invented that dodge of putting them right over on the far side of the table as soon as she'd swallowed her regular dose. Anyway, the point was that the oversight hadn't done her any serious harm and, if three should be one too many, she'd got the whole day to sleep it off.

So he had stirred them all into the very strong, very

sugary cocoa and she'd looked so sweet and relaxed, and sounded so grateful when he took it up to her. So pretty too, without those ghastly rollers and grease all over her face. Just for the moment, and quite illogically, he'd been on the point of advising her that it might be better not to drink quite all of it. He was glad now that he hadn't, though. Bob had been right and he felt as fit as a fiddle this morning.

At half past eight he went downstairs and let Nanki-Pooh out for a run in the garden, then filled the kettle and put two slices of bread in the toaster. He always liked to get to the supermarket early, before the queues started to grow at the check-outs, so while he was eating his breakfast he made a careful inspection of the store cupboard and refrigerator and then wrote his weekend shopping list, adding LAUNDERETTE in big letters under the last item.

It was half past ten when he got home from the supermarket and he could tell from the orderly state of the kitchen that Angie had not yet surfaced. However, this did not disturb him in the least because she very often slept until mid-day, or even later, on Saturdays and Sundays. So, when he had unpacked the shopping basket and stacked everything neatly away in its right place, he left a note for her on the kitchen table and then took Nanki's harness and lead off their hook on the back door, in preparation for an invigorating stroll along the beach.

The house was silent and the note just as he had left it when he returned at twelve o'clock and while he was getting the lunch ready he planned a little joke. He would put it on a tray and take it upstairs to the bedroom, making a fair amount of noise about it, so that she would wake up, give a mighty yawn and ask him what time it was.

'Breakfast time,' he'd say. 'Getting on for eight

o'clock!' Then, just as she was starting to bawl him out, he'd whip off the napkin which covered the tray, and lo! two lamb cutlets, new potatoes, petits pois and a glass of red wine.

The joke misfired, however, because when he was half way up the stairs, moving very cautiously so as not to spill a single drop of wine, he heard a sound which caused his hand to jerk and the glass to tip over and crash against a plate. Nanki-Pooh was crouched by the bedroom door, quivering like a jelly and whimpering in a way which sounded uncannily, horrifyingly like a human being.

He had never been more frightened in his life, not even in the war, and almost ten minutes went by before he could force himself to open the door.

'I just can't believe it,' Jane said, putting down the local paper, which had reported the inquest in full. 'It's simply incredible! Don't you find it incredible, Bob? I mean, to think that only a week ago they were here, in this very room, having dinner with us!'

'I suppose that's no guarantee of immortality,' Bob said, being a bit of a wag, and never more waggish than when seriously uneasy.

'But, joking apart, would you ever have dreamt that such a thing could happen? Did you get a clue that things were so terribly wrong?'

'Oh, most certainly I did,' he replied emphatically, seizing this chance to convince them both. 'She looked perfectly terrible that evening. You said so yourself, as soon as they'd gone.'

'Yes, I know, awfully tired and drawn, and she had her troubles, poor dear, but not all that unhappy, surely? Not suicidal, at any rate.'

'Oh, couldn't tell you, really,' Bob said. 'Hard for an outsider to judge, I should say, in cases of this sort.'

He was aware that his words were practically

meaningless and the reason for his deep uneasiness was that he was still cursing himself for not having taken Tony's protestations seriously. All that talk about how Angie would break her heart and worry herself to death if she were to be abandoned in her double bed had sounded so much like the maunderings of a senile and complacent husband that he had been fooled into suggesting that cheap and fatuous remedy. How the hell was he to know that it was the literal truth, that her confidence was so shaky that this tiny act of neglect would drive her to suicide? Still less that, unable to live with his remorse, Tony would put a revolver to his head, having first polished off that ridiculous Peke, of all macabre ideas! It made him feel like a bloody mass murderer, it really did. However, there was one thing his mind was made up about, and once again he repeated the solemn, silent vow he had made with himself.

'What's he so panicky about, I wonder?' Jane asked herself, watching him carry his empty glass over to the whisky bottle for the third time in half an hour; then lost the urge to speculate about his problems while still submerged in her own and, speaking aloud now, she uttered in almost identical terms the same solemn vow:

'Well, let it be a lesson to us never to hand out advice, however much we may be tempted. We can never know what untold havoc we may cause.'

'For Christ's sake, how did you . . . ?' Bob said, then checked himself too late, as he realised that she was sitting forward, with hands clasped and staring into the empty grate and that her words had been addressed to herself, rather than to him.

There was a longish silence, while the first small question marks of guilt began to hover between them, which were ultimately to do so much to damage what had hitherto been a perfectly decent marriage.

George Sims

FAMILY BUTCHER

Pasterne is arguably the prettiest village in the Hambleden valley. Skirmett, Frieth, Fingest and Ibstone all have their attractions as does Hambleden itself, and Turville is surmounted by a delightful windmill perched on a hill-top, a rarity indeed in the Chilterns, but Pasterne most conforms to a picture postcard village. There is the large green, immaculately trimmed, known as Pasterne Pound, with carefully preserved oak stocks, and a dozen brick and flint cottages grouped round the green just as if some Edwardian water colourist had placed them there for a painting. The village pond is a fine example too, kept fresh by a spring, with white ducks and mallard, and occasionally a nesting pair of swans. Postcards on sale in the village stores-cum-Post Office sell well in the summer months, particularly those featuring the pond and the rather eccentrically placed Norman church which appears to have turned its back on Pasterne due to its being the sole relic of an even earlier settlement. But people in picture postcard villages live lives much the same as the rest of us.

Another popular view of the village shows a northern aspect of the Pound with Daniel Patchin's butcher shop centrally placed, together with his Pound Cottage and the copse which hides Lord Benningworth's Manor House. Patchin's shop was originally an Elizabethan cottage that has been a good deal refurbished over the centuries, but the exterior, apart from the small shop window, must appear much as it did originally with its massive black oak beams and the plaster walls that are freshly white-washed each year. The name Daniel Patchin is in large white italic letters on the black façade, together with the trade description Family Butcher in smaller capitals.

Patchin's ancient establishment and the Post Office Stores are the only village shops: both are attractive and 'quaint', looking rather like the toy shops favoured by children of less sophisticated epochs. And Patchin's shop too is a model one for he is fanatical about personal cleanliness and hygiene: he wears a fresh apron twice a day, and the wash-basin at the rear of the shop is much used but kept spotless as are the display area and the large bench where Patchin works, 'looking more like a surgeon than a butcher', as Lord Benningworth once described him to some friends. Patchin's shop window always has a sparse display: a brace of pheasants, which he may well have shot himself, a hare, a local chicken or two, and one specimen of the prime meat he has for sale. Inside the shop there is a similarly small amount of meat on show: very likely just a side of Scotch beef hanging up with a Welsh shoulder of lamb. Under the impeccable refrigerated display counter there will be some of the famous Patchin sausages. Anything else that is required Daniel Patchin will have to fetch from the large cold room which takes up most of the rear portion of the shop.

The same shop when run by Daniel's father Gabriel was well known throughout the Chilterns in the 1930s, as was Reuben Patchin's before that: Daniel Patchin has an equally enviable reputation. Though the population of the village is not large enough to support such a thriving business, and Lord Benningworth who owns most of the village and the surrounding land is against more houses being built locally, callers come regularly from High Wycombe, Henley and Marlow for their meat. The Patchin sausages are still made exactly as detailed in Reuben's 1912 recipe with generous amounts of pork, herbs, spices and freshly ground black pepper; they bear no resemblance at all to the products churned out in factories, and they attract customers from as far away as Slough and Oxford.

Daniel Patchin, a quiet, sometimes taciturn man, is widely respected. He seems to live for his work and is busy throughout a long day for five and a half days each week. Wednesday is early closing and that afternoon he devotes to either fishing or shooting according to the season. When he returned from the Korean war Daniel Patchin came to an amicable unwritten agreement with Lord Benningworth that on Sundays he would act as an unpaid forester for the estate, keeping Benningworth's copses and woodland in good order, felling all diseased trees and clearing undergrowth, in return for which service he was allowed to keep all the timber he wanted. Every Sunday is devoted to this occupation and Patchin has a wood-yard at the back of his cottage where villagers can purchase logs and firewood.

The Patchin family has lived in Pasterne for centuries but the Benningworth connection with the locality is even more ancient: Lord Benningworth can trace his ancestry back in this country to a Baron Will de Benningworth in 1220, and there are stone effigies of another Benningworth Knight and his Lady installed in the church in 1290. The churchyard also houses many Patchin graves, but the earliest is dated 1695 with the epitaph:

> Good people all as you
> Pas by looke round
> See how Corpes' do lye
> For as you are som time Ware We
> and as we are so must you be

Occasionally in an evening Daniel Patchin may stroll

round the churchyard, eyeing the graves, particularly those of his own family. He likes those epitaphs which hint of un-Christian attitudes for he has a cynical, mordant sense of humour; he is not a church-goer. During his army service in Korea he found out that human life there was as cheap as that of turkeys at Christmas and he adopted a stoic's attitude to life and death. Serving as an infantryman he was awarded the Military Medal for his bravery in hand-to-hand fighting and won the nick-name 'Pig-sticker' from his comrades for his skill with the bayonet.

Daniel Patchin leads a very quiet life, devoted to work and country pursuits including gardening in the evenings. Lord Benningworth will sometimes stroll to the edge of his copse with a friend to point out Patchin's garden with its fine rose-beds and lines of potatoes, peas and beans as straight as guardsmen on parade. Patchin's wife Angela is ten years younger than him and before the marriage was known as a pretty, jolly and slightly flighty girl in Skirmett where she was brought up in a large farming family. The Patchins have no children as Angela proved to be barren, and over the ten years of marriage she has taken on the Patchin family's traits of seriousness and quiet outward mildness. She is a natural blonde with very fair, clear skin who blushes easily: any compliment from Benningworth's son and heir before he left to work in America would always make her change colour. She works behind the till in a cubicle-like office in the shop on Patchin's busiest days, always on Friday and Saturday, and occasionally on Thursday. Patchin employs a boy who makes himself generally useful on Friday evenings and Saturday mornings, otherwise he does all the work himself. He is a stocky man with massive muscles, enormously strong. Behind the shop there is a large shed which was used for all the slaughtering for the business up till about twenty years ago, and that is where Patchin despatches local poultry and scores of turkeys and geese at Christmas.

It was on a glorious late May afternoon that Daniel Patchin first became suspicious of his wife. It was a Monday and at lunch she had said that she would go for a walk in the afternoon. Returning at five she looked in at the shop to ask if he would like a cup of tea. He nodded and asked if she had enjoyed the walk. She hesitated and he looked up from the mincing machine to see that she had blushed and was nervously fiddling with the buttons on her blouse as if to make sure they were all fastened. It would be difficult to imagine a more observant man than Daniel Patchin: his whole life both at work and during his time away from the shop had sharpened his perceptions. He had made a life-time study of his customers and of nature; it was his sole inactive hobby. The slightest change in a pensioner's expression, even the movement of an eye, was enough to tell Patchin that he was proffering a too expensive piece of meat; the faintest ripple at the end of a roach 'swim' caught his notice as did the sound of a twig snapping. When she did not reply about the obvious pleasures of a country walk on a perfect May afternoon, Patchin covered his wife's loss for words with a quick comment about an old woman who always called in for broth bones on a Monday.

When Angela left the shop Patchin gave her back an intense look, noting that she had changed completely from the clothes she had worn at lunch. When she returned with the tray of tea she had covered her pretty white blouse with an old brown cardigan. She was still nervous, restless, very slightly ill at ease. Patchin knew that she was a hopeless liar but did not ask any more questions. There was a fresh smell of lemon soap and Patchin knew she had washed her face, probably plunging it repeatedly into cold water to get rid of the faint, pink flush. Again he covered her silence with talk of how he might go down to the river that evening. The season for coarse fishing did not start till mid-June but it was something he occasionally did out of season, inspecting favourite angling haunts to see how they had been affected by the high level of the Thames in winter.

During the next few weeks he added to his short list of pastimes the one of observing his wife: nothing that she did escaped him, even the merest hint of exasperation or frustration was filed away silently in his head – but nothing unusual ever attracted a comment from him.

It would not have required special ability as an observer to note Angela Patchin's revived interest in her clothes; even on Monday mornings when she did her weekly wash and on Wednesdays when she usually cleaned Pound Cottage from top to bottom she stopped wearing her old navy skirt and blossomed out in a new green one worn with a pretty apron, or jeans. She went to the Marks and Spencer store in Reading ostensibly to buy a summer frock but returned with several packages.

One Monday afternoon when Angela had gone for another walk Patchin closed the shop for a quarter of an hour and thoroughly inspected her chest of drawers. He took meticulous care in moving and replacing the various things; he found several new items of underwear including a particularly skimpy pair of knickers and a brassière designed to thrust size thirty-six breasts up and outwards as if proffering them to some lusty lad in a Restoration play. But which lusty lad? – that was the question that teased Daniel Patchin's brain, taking his attention away from his work so that he tended for the first time in his life to become a little absent-minded and not quite the usual model of efficiency. It was immediately noted by the villagers – 'Seems more human somehow', was the general verdict though expressed in different ways.

For a while Patchin speculated as to whether Lord Benningworth's son had returned to Pasterne and was again flattering Angela: if so it seemed a more serious matter than before, now apparently extending to her amply filled blouse. But an inquiry, casually phrased, to the Benningworth's housekeeper informed Patchin that the heir to the estate was still working happily in New York and did not plan to return home before Christmas.

Patchin's reaction to Angela's unusual behaviour varied considerably. At times he became quite fascinated by his secret observation in a detached way, as he had once studied an elusive old pike in a pool near Hambleden Mill: for weeks throughout one autumn he had tried various baits to entice the wily monster until he realised that the pike could be stirred into action only by a fish with fresh blood on it; so Patchin had served up a dace, liberally doused in blood, and the pike had succumbed. At other times Patchin experienced a feeling of cold fury that someone was stealing his wife from him – he was quite certain that it was happening. Once he woke with a horrid start in the middle of the night convinced that the telephone had rung just once, and then lay awake consumed with feelings of jealousy and twisted lust – he did not fall asleep till just before the alarm bell rang at six.

Perhaps Angela's changed attitude to sex was the most obvious give-away. Before the Monday afternoon walks and the new clothes she seemed to have regarded it as a rather boring routine matter to be managed as quickly as possible before turning away to sleep. Now she never turned away and was always ready for sex, keener than he could ever remember her being. Her kisses were open-mouthed and lingering, her embraces passionate and urgent – as he brooded on this he realised that 'urgent' was the key word – that was it, she was urging him on to more effort so that he re-

144

sembled, when her eyes were closed, her other, very passionate lover. Even after an orgasm she was unsatisfied, longing for something else. It would be impossible to describe the various feelings Patchin experienced as his wife became ever more knowing in bed, with wanton behaviour and explicit movements trying to get him to obtain the results she enjoyed elsewhere. One night she wanted him to make love in a new position and as she determinedly pushed him into place he could see the grim joke of it so clearly that he nearly laughed. Nothing could make it more plain that Angela had a very virile, enthusiastic lover, much more skilled at the amatory arts than he would ever be; a lover who liked first to be inflamed by skimpy knickers and a 'display' brassière and then performed perfectly.

It was not until a Friday in the middle of June that Patchin was able to identify his cuckold enemy. He disturbed Angela while she was making a phone call when he entered Pound Cottage that lunch time a few minutes earlier than usual. As he opened the door the telephone was slammed down and Angela ran upstairs to cover her confusion. That afternoon Ray Johnson, the youngest postman in the area, called in at the shop ostensibly for a pound of sausages and some bacon. Johnson grinned over at Angela in the little office, calling out: 'Afternoon Mrs Patchin.' Angela did not reply but just nodded, flushing very slightly. Apart from that tell-tale flush there was something subtle about the way Johnson addressed her, with just an inflection of the 'Mrs Patchin', as though the formal mode of address was something of a joke between the pair. Daniel Patchin took his time in the cold storage room to give them a chance for a few words. The moment he opened the door Ray Johnson stopped talking and grinned foolishly as though he had forgotten what he was going to say.

Idiot, Patchin thought, you young idiot, but passed

145

over the momentary awkwardness for Johnson by commenting on the sausages: 'Cook's specials this lot. Part of a batch I made up for the Manor. The old man likes just an extra pinch of pepper.'

Having once seen his wife with Johnson there was no longer any doubt in Patchin's mind, for it seemed to him as if there was some invisible but subtly tangible connection between them, an unspoken intimacy born of their long afternoons together, probably in Calcot Wood where there were some idyllic glades. As he did up the bacon and sausages and the embarrassed couple said nothing Patchin could visualise them on a green sward in a patch of dappled sunlight – the flimsy knickers being removed together with the trick brassière – and then Angela's urgent movements as the mutual madness began. Patchin felt as though his obsessive thoughts might show on his usually phlegmatic face so he cleared his throat loudly and shook his head, saying 'Sorry. Throat's a bit sore. Hope it's not a summer cold.'

Ray Johnson gave Patchin an unusually serious, not altogether friendly look as he replied, 'Yes. Let's hope not.' The look negated the banal response and Patchin thought: Liar. It would please you if I came down with pneumonia. For the first time it struck him that the feeling of jealousy might not all be on one side. Probably Johnson was also jealous, of the nights when Patchin slept with Angela; possibly Johnson was coming to hate him as he had hated the unknown lover.

Later that afternoon, when Angela had gone back to the cottage to make some tea, Daniel Patchin stood at the open door of the shop staring at the pond where a pair of Canada geese had alighted and were being harried and made unwelcome by the aggressive though small coots which dashed in and out of the reeds, making proprietorial noises. And indeed Patchin did not miss anything that happened on the pond, noting how the mallards vanished and the white ducks kept out of the noisy quarrel like only faintly interested spectators. But Patchin's mind was elsewhere, brooding on his predicament: it was the first time since the Korean war that Patchin felt he was faced with a problem he did not know how to handle. Ray Johnson was a tall slight lad with curly black hair and a mouth that always seemed to be open, either grinning or laughing to show very white teeth. Johnson was easily the most popular of the local postmen; he was extremely cheerful, full of banter and old jokes. Patchin had always found that slightly irritating – but now the trifling feeling of irritation was replaced by the strong one of implacable enmity. Patchin had no intention of confronting Angela with his suspicions or of trying to surprise the lovers in the act, even though he thought it could be arranged one Monday afternoon in Calcot Wood. For all he knew Angela might then decide to leave him – he did not know how heavily their reasonably prosperous and comfortable life together weighed against the hours of passion spent with Lothario Johnson. No, the only answer was to get rid of him as the coots would undoubtedly rid themselves of the intruding Canada geese.

After the break for tea Patchin got down to work again. Friday evening was one of his busiest times as dozens of joints had to be prepared for the weekend – he had some particularly choosy customers who liked to have their meat prepared in the finicky French manner and he was quite willing to cater to their tastes. A great deal of beef had been ordered for that weekend and his young assistant was not up to preparing it, being capable of carrying out only the humblest jobs. Patchin set the boy to mincing pork and then began butchering two sides of beef, attacking the carcase with relish.

Once supper was finished he could hardly wait to get Angela to bed: knowing that she was the young man's mistress had the strange, unexpected effect of doubling his lust for her. And she seemed equally ready for sex, falling back on the bed and raising her knees, smiling at him in a new way, a smile that contained a hint of amusement at his fumbling efforts to please her. This time it was his turn to be left feeling unsatisfied and empty even though he took her twice, as if possessing her half a dozen times would not be enough to assuage his restless yearning.

From mid-June Daniel Patchin spent most of his Sundays in Calcot Wood – it was by far the largest area of woodland owned by Lord Benningworth. One Sunday he decided to devote to searching for clues as to the lovers' meeting-place and did come on a bed of crushed ferns with a strange sensation that left him feeling slightly sick. From the improvised bed he made his way down to a deserted cottage in the remotest part of the wood, a spot that never seemed to be reached by the sun as it stood in the shadow of Calcot Hill. It had been a game-keeper's cottage up to 1939 but the pre-war Benningworth regime of having a game-keeper had been dropped and the remote, unattractive cottage was let, when Patchin was a youth, to a strange old man called Ted Ames, then left to rot. Lord Benningworth was a true conservative in that he was against change of any kind, even that of having a wreck of a building knocked down. The old widower Ames had eventually gone off his head and been taken away to a mental hospital in 1948, where he died. Since then the cottage had been stripped of its gutters and drain-pipes; most of the roof was still sound but rain had dripped in through a few missing tiles and some of the rafters were rotten, covered in mould: even on the warmest summer day the old cottage smelt of dank decay. There was fungus on the kitchen walls and weeds were gradually invading the ground floor rooms, sprouting up from the cracks in the brick floors.

Daniel Patchin stood absolutely still for a long while staring at the ruined building which some villagers claimed was haunted by Ted Ames. Patchin did not believe in ghosts, spirits, Heaven or Hell: he believed that the Universe was incomprehensible and absolutely indifferent to mankind. Suddenly he said aloud: 'What a waste. Pity not to make some use of the old place.' The second sentence, spoken in a particularly mild voice, ended on a faintly questioning note and for the first time he moved his head as though he were talking to someone and waiting for a comment on his suggestion. Then he gave the idea engendered by his memory of a certain feature of the ancient fireplace in Ames's kitchen a mirthless smile and turned on his heel.

Throughout Calcot Wood there were piles of logs that Patchin built till he was ready to remove a truckload. There was also a hut where he kept a chain-saw, tins of petrol, axes and bags of wood chips and sawdust. He looked around to make sure that there was no one about, and began to carry sacks of sawdust and chippings over to the cottage; he felt a great satisfaction in commencing work on his plan.

On succeeding Sundays Daniel Patchin spent a good deal of time in transporting dry branches and brushwood; he also used his van to move cans of paraffin, half-empty tins of paint, plastic bags that had contained dripping, sacks of fat, soiled rags and other rubbish. These he carefully planted throughout the cottage, gradually turning it into a massive bonfire.

While the preparations in Calcot Wood were proceeding satisfactorily Patchin made a study of Ray Johnson's working life. By casual questions to the village Postmistress, who delighted in gossip, he wormed out the routine of Johnson and other postmen in the area. One of his discoveries was that Johnson often had either Monday or Wednesday afternoon off, and this was confirmed for him on the first Wednesday in July when Angela took a surprising interest in his fishing plans for that afternoon. Usually she was bored by angling so he answered these questions with concealed, wry humour. Then, prompted by a whim, he took more time than usual in his preparations for the weekly expedition to the Thames. His fishing equipment was the simplest that could be devised – he despised the 'London crowd' who invaded the river at weekends weighed down with paraphernalia. He had an all-purpose rod, a few hooks and floats and one reel carried in an army haversack. As he pretended to fuss over these things, and to take an unusually long time in making the flour paste for bait, he could see that Angela was very much on edge, nervous and yet pleasurably excited at the same time. She had not mentioned going out so he suspected that there might be a plan for Johnson to visit Pound Cottage while he was away: 'While the cat's away the mice will play,' he said over and over in his mind as he rolled the ball of dough between his strong, dry fingers.

When he at last set off in the van he was again ironically amused that Angela came out to wave goodbye as though to be certain of his departure. Patchin spent an hour on the river-bank but was not in the mood for fishing. The reeds were haunted by colourful dragon-flies and there was a brief darting visit from a kingfisher – sights that usually pleased him, but on this occasion he was hardly aware of anything about him, feeling rather like a ghost returned to haunt the scene of past pleasures.

Patchin drove back from the Thames with not much heart for what lay immediately ahead, but he now felt it was essential to make quite sure of the situation. In Pasterne he parked his van by the pond and appeared to stare down into its clear water for a while. Such behaviour on his part would not excite comment for he had been known to catch stickle-backs and frogs there to use as bait when angling for pike.

After some minutes of staring with unseeing eyes Patchin ambled back to his closed shop, then walked through it into the garden that led up to Pound Cottage. He trod noiselessly over the lawn and entered the side door very quietly. Within a minute his suspicions were dramatically confirmed: through the board ceiling that separated the living-room from the bedroom he heard the squeaking springs of his double bed, squeaking so loudly that it seemed as if the springs were protesting at the extraordinary behaviour of the adulterous couple. Then there began a peculiar rhythmical grunting noise and his wife called out something incomprehensible in a strange voice.

Patchin retreated noiselessly, got back into his car and returned to Hambleden Mill. He fished stolidly for three hours with a dour expression on his face – an expression that some North Korean soldiers had probably glimpsed before he killed them with his bayonet. Usually he returned small fish to the river but on that afternoon he just ripped them off the hook and threw them on the bank.

Returning home again at about his usual time, Patchin found his wife in an excellent mood. Fornication seemed to be good for her health as she appeared blooming. A delicious supper had been prepared for him and Angela had popped over to the village stores to buy a bottle of the dry cider he favoured. She looked quite fetching with her flushed cheeks, her curly blond hair freshly washed, and the two top buttons of a new pink blouse left undone, but Patchin could not respond at all; momentarily he found it difficult to keep up the pretence of not knowing about her affair and felt as though an expression of suspicion and cold contempt must appear on his face. When he went to wash he stared in the mirror and was surprised to find the usual phlegmatic expression reflected.

After supper Angela wanted to stroll around in the garden. It was something Patchin normally enjoyed, seeing the results of all his hard work, for in July the garden looked at its best with the rose-beds 'a picture' as Angela said, and usually it was very satisfactory to inspect the neat rows of vegetables. Instead he experienced a most unusual mood of emptiness and frustration – everything seemed hollow and meaningless.

While his wife bent down to smell a rose Daniel Patchin stared up at the clear evening sky. He knew his enjoyment of life was temporarily lost, and that it would not return until he was rid of the man who threatened his marriage. Angela came and stood by him, took his hand and placed it on her firm round breast, an action that would have been quite out of character a few months before; but her new sensuality did not move him at all, and when they went to bed making love to her was like a ritual, quite spoilt by his memory of the protesting bed-springs.

Patchin decided to try to put his plan of murder into effect on the second Wednesday in July. Angela went for a walk again on the Monday of that week, so according to his understanding of the postman's routine it seemed probable that Ray Johnson would be working on the Wednesday afternoon. If so he would then be driving down the narrow lane that skirted Calcot Wood to clear a remote, little-used post-box at about 3 p.m.

On the Wednesday Patchin felt quite calm and confident that everything would go as he devised. He set off from Pound Cottage promptly at 2 p.m. after an excellent lunch of roast loin of pork with the first new potatoes from the garden and a large helping of broad beans. His haversack had been got ready on the previous evening: it now contained some other things as well as fishing tackle – rubber gloves, matches, a ball of extremely tough cord, sticking plasters and a foot long piece of iron pipe.

Parking his van just off the lane by the wood in a cunningly chosen spot where it would not be seen, Patchin took his haversack and walked quickly through the wood to Ames's cottage. He experienced pleasurable excitement in doing so and in inspecting the fire he had laid in the kitchen grate. It consisted of three fire-lighters, paper spills and wood chippings, a few sticks and numerous small pieces of coal. It had been constructed with the care that a chaffinch gives to making its nest, and he estimated that it would burn intensely for an hour or two. 'Quite long enough to roast a joint,' he said in an expressionless voice as he got up from his crouching position in front of the grate.

After inspecting the trails of wood chippings soaked in paraffin which he had laid throughout the cottage like long fuses leading to explosive charges, he glanced round the wildly overgrown plot that had once been a garden. Rank grass a foot high contended with massive clumps of nettles, giant docks and cow parsley. He did not think that it would be possible to trace foot-prints on such a terrain, but also he did not expect his enterprise to be risk-free. There were bound to be risks in a life governed by mere chance.

It was 2.45 p.m. when he walked back through the wood to the narrow, twisting lane. He wore the rubber gloves with his left hand in his old fishing-jacket pocket and the other plunged into the haversack that hung from his right shoulder. He positioned himself in the lane so that he would be on the driver's side of the van when it approached him. The oppressive mood which had dogged him for so many weeks had lifted and he whistled as he waited – a rather tuneless version of *As time goes by* which he repeated over and over again.

At 3 p.m. precisely he heard a motor engine in the lane and got ready to wave the van down if it was driven by Johnson. For the first time that afternoon excitement seized him, with a thumping of his heart and a sudden tremor of fear such as he had always experienced before hand-to-hand fighting in Korea. He had once said to another soldier there: 'Everyone's afraid at times. Anyone who says he isn't is either a liar or a fool.'

As the Post Office van came round the corner Patchin waved it down, first tentatively then more vigorously as he spotted Johnson's head of black curly hair. Johnson stopped the van, rolled its window further down and called out, 'What's up?'

Patchin walked slowly across to the van, limping very slightly and holding himself as though he was in pain. 'Sorry, sorry,' he said. 'Bit of trouble.' He came close to the van door and stood silent, with his eyes half-closed and swaying slightly as though he was going to faint.

With a puzzled expression in which there was just the faintest hint of suspicion Johnson opened the van door and began to get out – his height made doing so a rather awkward business. Patchin took out the iron pipe and hit Johnson on the head, a measured blow by someone who had considerable experience in stunning animals. Johnson lurched forward and then fell in a heap, just like a poleaxed bullock. Patchin bundled him back into the van, got into the driving seat and drove off down the lane, whistling the same tune again. After a hundred yards he turned off on to a track which led in the direction of the gamekeeper's cottage. Before leaving the red van he pressed Johnson's fingers on the steering-wheel, then bundled the body up and carried it on his shoulder as easily as he managed a side of beef.

He also paused in the decaying doorway to impress Johnson's fingerprints on two empty paraffin cans, and carried him through to the kitchen. The tall man was still inert, but as Patchin dropped his burden on to the cement floor Johnson's eyelids flickered. Patchin sat him up like a ventriloquist's dummy and then knocked him out with a blow to the jaw that would have floored most boxers.

Patchin put sticky plasters over Johnson's large mouth, then worked on the unconscious man with the skill he always showed in preparing joints. He put his legs neatly together and bound them tightly from above the knee to the ankles, using the same binding technique he used in repairing his fishing rod, pulling the cord so tight that the legs became immobile; he left a loop by the ankles. He repeated the process with the limp arms. Then came the part that gave him most satisfaction: lifting the two loops on to the hooks that had once supported a turn-spit in front of the fire. Immediately Johnson was suspended like an animal carcase ready to be roasted, Patchin lit the fire in the grate and left the cottage.

Before taking off his rubber gloves Patchin picked up the empty paraffin cans and left them near the old garden gate which was half hanging off its hinges, then strode off to the place where he had hidden his own van. The time was 3.30 and everything had gone exactly as he had hoped. There was always blind chance of course – for instance the remote possibility that another pair of lovers might be trespassing in the woods and see him striding along so purposefully, but there was nothing he could do about it.

Driving to the Thames, Patchin mentally examined his plan again and formulated one or two more things to be done. As soon as he had parked the van near Hambleden Mill he assembled his rod and line right down to putting on the bait, a thing he never did till he was actually on the river bank, so that anyone seeing him might think he had already been fishing and was trying another spot. Then, carrying the assembled rod, he walked along the gravel path and over the complicated series of weirs which cross the Thames at Hambleden Mill. As he approached the lock he watched to see whether the keeper there might be in sight and was relieved to be able to cross unseen.

Patchin threw his piece of iron pipe into the river before spending an hour angling: he fished like a young boy, close in to the bank where there were more bites to be had but the fish were always small. He caught a tiny roach and three gudgeon but was quite satisfied with them, leaving the last gudgeon on the hook as he walked back to the lock. Good fortune was still with him for the lock-keeper was now at work opening the gates for a motor cruiser. The keeper, who knew Patchin well, called out 'Any luck Dan?'

'Not much. Just tiddlers,' Patchin called out, shaking his rod so that the suspended gudgeon twisted about at the end of the line. 'Think I'll use them to try for a pike in the pool by the mill. See you.'

'Yes, see you. Will you keep me a nice small chicken for the weekend?'

'Yes. Right.' Patchin walked off just fractionally quicker than he did normally. With excitement working in him at the prospect of revisiting Ames's cottage it was not easy to appear just as usual. For once he was grateful that he had a rather expressionless face.

His mind on other things, he mechanically dismantled the fishing rod and line as quickly as he could. 'Yes, all going to plan,' he said aloud though there was no one within a hundred yards of him.

Driving back to the lane once more he experienced a surprising feeling of let-down and anti-climax. It was true that it had all gone without a hitch as far as he could tell, but somehow it seemed a bit too easy. There would have been more satisfaction if he could have allowed the tall but puny Johnson a chance to fight, some ludicrous attempt at self-defence which he would have brushed away derisively, as easily as a tom-cat deals with a rat.

Once in Calcot Wood again Patchin's nose twitched. There was a faint aroma like that of roast pork which had greeted him at lunch time at Pound Cottage. It grew stronger at every step he took. Desultory grey fumes struggled up from the ancient chimney. The smell was very strong in the hall and unpleasantly so in the kitchen which reeked of cooking odours and where a blackened, twisted carcase was still roasting and dripping fat into a dying fire.

Despite the smell Patchin stayed there looking at the object which bore no resemblance to the once garrulous postman. Patchin's hatred of the man had quite disappeared now that there was no longer any need for it – he was not gloating over his victim, but musing on the quintessential evanescence of man. How easily was man humbled, how soon was he changed into rotting meat! It had been just the same in Korea: one minute his friend 'Dusty' Seddon had been telling a dirty joke, the next moment lying mute with most of his face blown off.

Pausing in the hall, Patchin set light to a pile of paraffin-soaked sawdust and then lit the trails of wood-chips and retreated to the sagging front door, throwing the box of matches behind him.

The fire had taken a firm grip on the cottage before Patchin had even left the garden; he could hear it raging and roaring unseen until a sheet of flame sprang up at one of the diamond-leaded windows. For the second time that day Patchin experienced a slight attack of nerves; momentarily his right hand shook and for a few minutes he seemed to be walking on lifeless legs, having to make an extraordinary amount of effort just to propel himself along.

Seated in his van Patchin took out a large hand-kerchief and wiped his forehead which was sweating profusely, and allowed himself a few minutes rest before driving off in his customary careful manner. Was there something he had overlooked – perhaps a trifling slip which might lead the police to his door in a few days' time? As he navigated a series of lanes and minor roads that would put him once again on the main road from Hambleden to Pasterne, his mind was exercised by the nagging suspicion that he might have made one vital mistake.

Calm gradually returned as he drove slowly along, and he began to think of the possible effect of the fire on the Benningworth estate. The large garden of rank grass and weeds should act as a barrier between the fire and Calcot Wood, but even if it did spread then Lord Benningworth owed him a favour for all the hard work he had put in there as amateur forester for twenty-five years. A sudden thought made Patchin smile. The Benningworth family motto *Esse quam videri*, 'To be rather than to seem to be', was well known in the locality; it was a pity that Ray Johnson had not known that Daniel Patchin also had a motto: 'What I have I hold'.

When Patchin arrived in Pasterne he felt completely normal. His pleasant life had been momentarily threatened with an upheaval but that was now all over. The village looked particularly lovely in the late afternoon sunlight. The white ducks were sedulously paddling to and fro as though they were paid to do so, and swifts were skimming over the clear pond's mirror-like surface, occasionally dipping down to it, hunting midges. The Postmistress's black and white cat moved carefully over the neatly clipped grass as if it might be stalking a newt and sat down at the edge of the pond. 'Pretty as a picture,' Patchin said.

Walking along to Pound Cottage Daniel Patchin thought of what he should say when he saw Angela. It was essential to appear absolutely as normal so that when she heard of the perplexing tragedy in Calcot Wood nothing about his behaviour should prompt suspicion in her mind. Then he understood Angela's difficulty in appearing quite normal or saying anything about that walk she had taken on the glorious May afternoon because phrases that he went over in his mind seemed artificial and suspicious. 'Nice afternoon, but I didn't catch anything' – false. 'I enjoyed it, but not good fishing weather' – unnatural.

But Patchin need not have worried, for as soon as he opened the side door he heard the squeak of protesting bed-springs and Angela calling out in a voice that sounded false and unnatural.

Michael Sinclair

REPORT FROM SECTION NINE

It came first into the Minister's life on a cold, unsatis-
factory February morning. His Private Secretary rang
him at eight to say that the Prime Minister wanted a
brief word before Cabinet. The call had resulted in
burnt toast, cold coffee and no BBC news headlines.
The phone rang again: his driver telling him that the
Rover had broken down, and that there would be an
hour's delay. Cup of coffee in one hand, he went through
to his study and unlocked the battered despatch box.
He would have worked through his correspondence
files the night before, but, with his wife away in the
constituency, he had spent too long with Lara. Too long
and too much to drink. He was not in the best of
condition to start the day with little problems; irritation
welled within him, looking for an outlet.

Expiation of sins . . . extra long hours . . . clear up
the backlog . . . He'd always been like that: self-
administered confessional followed by self-imposed
penances. He'd make a firm start. Sitting at his desk he
opened the box and picked up the first paper. Right on
top *Report from Section Nine: Secret.* He'd seen many like it
before. Its tight wording was to the point: The Patriotic
Movement, the so-called L.F.G., had him on their list.
There was nothing intrinsically surprising in that. In
his position, with his present role in the Peace
Negotiations . . . Even so, within his icy self, he felt a
chill, the sort of fear that dragged him back twenty

years to a cold dark night in the Troödos Mountains in Cyprus; the National Service second Lieutenant and the equally young EOKA terrorist, who had come face to face under the lee of a high cliff. He sat awhile, holding tight to himself, then, regaining control, he put aside the Report from Section Nine and got down to work.

His wife rang. Why was he not at the office? He explained, but knew that she was still suspicious. 'Ring the bloody car pool if you don't believe me,' he wanted to shout, but did not. He must avoid another row today. Besides it was true. His story was true. She . . . did his wife really believe he'd bring someone to the flat . . . that he'd be so foolish? Did she know . . . ? How could she know about Lara?

'Hope you don't find the Institute lunch too boring, dear,' he said brightly. 'See you late tonight. Yes . . . midnight at least . . . Bye . . .'

Back to desk and files. A brief from the office was next, on prospects from the new round of Geneva Peace Talks. It was only a month since he'd returned from the last session, press and TV praising him to heaven, saying he'd achieved a break-through. He'd known then that it was only window-dressing, that it would fall to pieces as soon as the two delegations got back home. It had, and the L.F.G. was jubilant. He'd been blamed for not following up his success. The bloody press were so fickle. They knew nothing. He carefully laid the brief aside, on top of the Report from Section Nine.

Good: a bundle of straight-forward letters to constituents for his signature: *Dear Mrs Smith, I am sorry that you have had so much trouble with your dog licence and am forwarding your letter to the appropriate government department asking them to look into the matter . . .*

Christ . . . that new secretary. Useless typist . . . A mistake on every line. If he could get his dictation right, why the hell couldn't she do a neat job? Well he wasn't going to send out letters in that condition, not even to constituents. She'd have to do the lot again or get out. There were plenty of other girls who'd jump at the chance . . . and prettier. That's how he'd first found Lara. She'd resigned; it could have become embarrassing otherwise. He'd kept her on on other terms. Lara . . . could his wife have found out about Lara . . . ? He piled the constituents' letters on top of the Geneva Peace Talks brief.

The Office had done a tight piece of work on the draft speech for the Foreign Press Association. Good, tough stuff. Full of optimism about the Talks. It underlined his refusal to consider having the L.F.G. represented. A bunch of thugs, terrorists, murderers, with no idea of what they wanted except chaos. He knew about terrorists. These ones were scarcely literate, representing no one but themselves. He was adamant; they hated him for it. For a brief moment he thought about the Report from Section Nine, but that morning, it was still a factor no bigger than a man's clenched fist.

The two hours' drive from the House of Commons to his constituency would relax him. Friday evening, a week's work well done and not much that looked liable to blow up over the weekend. And a pat on the back from the P.M. before Cabinet had killed the early frustrations of the day. He dozed in the back of the chauffeur-driven Rover. A late supper with his wife; they'd both be tired; a bottle of wine and a Saturday lie-in, followed by an hour's constituency work with his political agent, then gardening, see a few friends; a twenty-four hours unwind.

A very few friends. In the many press profiles of him that had appeared over the last years, the catch-words and phrases repeated themselves into hackneyed meaninglessness. 'A man of few personal friends; fewer still in the House or Government. But people recognise his worth, his foresight, his determination. And his physical courage . . . not many men of twenty-three were awarded the M.C. in so-called peace-time. Leading an anti-EOKA patrol, he had, single handed . . . A brilliant mind too . . . ambitious . . . arrogant . . . heartless . . . cold; listening to no one . . . listening only to the workings of his own mind. A man of many enemies – at home and on the world stage.'

Friends . . . ? Of course he had friends. Enemies . . . ? Well perhaps a few people disliked him. Cold . . . ? Let them ask Lara if he was cold or distant. And what was wrong with a touch of arrogance, if it was justified by performance?

He fell asleep in his seat, and when he awoke they were somewhere to the north of Hendon. His head couched back against the cushion, he lay in that twilight on the edge of consciousness, staring without perception at the neatly clipped hair on the back of his chauffeur's neck. He could distinguish such detail with unusual clarity in the glaring headlights from a car behind. As he drifted back to reality, he was aware that the other man was annoyed.

'Something the matter, Brigson?' he asked in a voice still slurred by sleep.

'Bastard sitting right up my tail.'

'Let him pass.'

'Tried that, sir. He just sticks behind. Playing silly buggers. Look at him now.'

The Minister craned his neck pointlessly to look behind into full-beamed headlights. Leaving suburbia on the approach road to the motorway, they were travelling at just over the fifty-five mark.

'I'll give 'im one more chance. If he don't lay off then, I'll pull on to the hard shoulder.'

A mile or so later, with no let-up from the car behind, the chauffeur pulled into the side. The other car pulled up as well, stopping some twenty-five yards away.

'I'll go, give them a choice piece of my language,' said the chauffeur, getting out carefully. With a lot of north-bound traffic, it would be an easy accident. The Minister waited and watched from the car.

'Careful if they're drunk,' he called, winding down his window. He wasn't worried. The driver was big; a powerful ex-policeman.

It happened quickly. The Minister watched it all through the rear window. The chauffeur got to within five yards of the vehicle which was standing with only its parking lights on. Then its motor burst into life, and, headlights suddenly blazing, it was driven straight at him. The chauffeur dived sideways down a grassy, litter-strewn bank, rolled over and lay still. That was all that the Minister had time to take in, for the car was now up, parallel with him. Two people were in the front. The nearside window was wound down and he could make out a face with something weirdly deformed about its features. Only later did he realise that the man had been wearing a stocking mask.

The door of the strange car was opening. In a spasm of panic, the Minister struggled to get out; this was something he had to get away from, defend himself from out in the open, not trapped in the rear seat. He was half way out when a huge articulated lorry, thundering up the inner lane of the motorway, pulled out too late and gave the rogue car a glancing blow along the driver's side. Metal screeched against metal. The lorry pulled up ahead, but by then, the car and its hooded occupants had plunged on into the night.

The Minister's chauffeur staggered up, bruised but otherwise unhurt; the driver of the lorry stalked back to find out what had happened and the Minister, clutching hard at the door-frame, heard out a remarkable twin vocabulary of invective directed at the departed car. A passing police patrol stopped and the story was retailed to them. They saluted respectfully when the

Minister identified himself and told them to report the incident to the Yard. Their talk was all of madmen and gangsters; the Minister kept to himself the ever-inflating memory of the Report from Section Nine.

But only the softest blush of menace was still with him by the time he arrived home. A peaceful drive of a hundred yards led to his house which was buried well back from the main road among the trees. All was in darkness. His wife would already be in bed. He said goodnight to his driver and started searching for his keys. Inside the front door he found the light-switch, then on the hall table a hastily written note from his wife. Her sister had had a stroke; she had gone to be with her. 'Cold meat and salad in the fridge. Ring me when you get home,' she ended.

He picked up the phone, and began to dial. The line was dead; totally dead. Swearing softly under his breath, he replaced the receiver and went and got himself some food and a wet whisky, then, for company, turned on the late television news. Threats of a new rail strike, an earthquake in Chile and a terrorist attack on the Lebanese Ambassador in Paris. He helped himself to another whisky. He would have argued that the incident on the motorway had made him curious rather than upset, but he'd had a hard week; he owed himself a second drink. He watched a late night movie – a hack Los Angeles crime story. Eventually, he relaxed.

It was different at three in the morning. He awoke to night noises for the wind had picked up. Childhood fears of the dark coursed through his mind. For a brief moment he remembered too what he had, over the twenty years, trained himself to forget. The moon riding high in a storm-battered sky. The uncontrollable emotion when his platoon, from whom he had in his panic been separated, had found him with the bodies strewn around him. The sound of weeping in the vale when, with his men bivouacked comfortingly around him, he woke in the damp dawn of the next day and saw below the beautiful girl kneeling by the body of the young terrorist.

The Minister lay awake for a long time, thinking on the motorway incident, the dead telephone and the Report from Section Nine. After a while he got up, turned the lights on, and walked round the house checking that all doors and windows were locked. Outside a gale was brewing and, around four, a crash came from downstairs followed by the sound of breaking glass. He froze in panic, quelling a childish compulsion to pull the blankets over his head and take to the safety of warm blackness. No further sound came from below, so, after five sweating minutes and with a heart that throbbed so loudly that it would deaden any stealthy footstep, he turned on every light he could find, seized a heavy bronze trophy from some long-forgotten tennis championship, and plunged resolutely downstairs. Dining room, sitting room, study, then the kitchen door, which resisted his gentle push. He thrust it open and a great wind forced him back into renewed terror. He saw, through the door, the gaping window where a large branch from an overhanging elm had projected itself into the room amid a pile of splintered glass. How often had his wife tried to persuade him to have that tree cut down; it was too close to the house.

He recovered himself, burying all his fears with activity. Putting on wellingtons, he removed the branch and found some board to nail over the hole in the window. Twice he cut himself on the broken glass. Then he returned to bed and slept fitfully till dawn.

Marooned as he was without car or telephone, he set off at around eight in the morning to walk the mile and a half to the village. It was raining softly but soon he felt refreshed, returning to his normal self after the interruptions of the night. Where the road passed ploughed fields lined by high hedgerows, two men suddenly appeared only yards in front of him. Both were carrying shotguns. He drew back in blind terror for the moments it took him to recognise gamekeepers from the neighbouring estate. They greeted him politely enough, but he felt them looking at him strangely as he went on his way. From then he moved quickly, at times almost breaking into a run, breath heaving through an aching chest. He fought back unreasoned panic and kept turning to see that no one was following him, jerking back once more in fear when a brace of grouse whirred close overhead. Just as he reached the security of the police station on that otherwise deserted Saturday, he saw his car approaching. His wife was driving.

'Hello Oliver,' she stopped and wound down the window. 'What are you doing?' The voice was calm.

'Coming to phone you. Thought you'd be worried that I didn't get in touch last night. Phone's out of order . . .' His words, in contrast, babbled out in breathless spate.

'That's why I came back. I couldn't get through to you either. They got Alice to hospital. She's not doing too badly . . .'

'Good,' he said. 'Good . . . Oh, that tree. Bad news I'm afraid, dear. Branch came down.' He clambered into the car beside his wife. 'Kitchen window . . .'

'I was right, Oliver. I told you a hundred times to have it cut.'

The weekend passed, tensions were gradually replaced by matrimonial squabble, and the Report from Section Nine returned to refuge in the recesses of his mind. The new week dawned. At first the only outward change in the abrasive life of the Minister was that, much to the surprise of the Commissioner who had long failed to persuade him of such necessity, a full-time police bodyguard suddenly became acceptable. The Minister composed a well-mannered memorandum on the subject, arguing that while he had no worries on his own account, he now felt that he owed it to the high office he held as one of Her Majesty's Ministers, to take account of the increasingly vicious realities of modern life. 'I have been prevailed upon . . .' he wrote; he did not specify how or by whom. That same day, the resolute and intelligent Inspector Trehayne of Special Branch was assigned to the post.

Thirty-six hours after his appointment, Inspector Trehayne reported his particular anxieties to his Chief Inspector. Together the two officers walked along the corridor to see the Superintendent. As the Chief Superintendent and his Divisional Commander were out on the ninth hole of the Police golf championship, the three men moved up to the Office of the Deputy Assistant Commissioner. The latter's advice was to sit on the problem and report back. It was a politically sensitive matter.

Trehayne's worries had little to do with the security of the Minister; on that score he had nothing untoward to report. He was, however, much concerned about the state of the Minister's mind. From having been cynical, unflappable, totally opposed to having a police guard, the Minister was now bombarding Inspector Trehayne with a barrage of requests, demands, orders relating to his own security. That low-level, routine, unconfirmed Report from Section Nine (and damn Section Nine for processing that particular report without more hard evidence, said the Commissioner to whom the problem had been elevated) now had become the fulcrum of the Minister's every moment.

The Private Secretary to the Minister also began to notice a change. He spoke to the Permanent Under-Secretary who had a word with the Secretary of the

Cabinet, Sir Lloyd Roberts. Sir Lloyd reluctantly way-laid the P.M. as he was going over to the House for Question Time.

'The Minister . . . forgive me for mentioning it, Prime Minister . . . that is . . . he appears to be under a bit of strain. Needs a couple of weeks off.'

'Nonsense Lloyd. He'll have to pull himself together. Can't have him falling apart right now, not with two by-elections next week. I'll talk to him. Sort him out quickish.'

'Very good, Prime Minister,' said Sir Lloyd Roberts meekly.

The Prime Minister either did not find the time or forgot to speak to the Minister and two more days passed. The change was rapid. The Minister took to shouting at people, even muttering to himself. He would break into a sweat. Then he started locking himself into his office, his bedroom . . .

The Minister's wife came up to London, ostensibly to do some shopping, but in fact to have a quiet word with the Chief Whip who was an old boyfriend. Her husband was behaving most oddly; couldn't sleep at night, felt people were watching him, that someone was after him the whole time. He kept mentioning a report, a report from something called Section Nine.

Twenty-four hours later, with the Minister safely at a dull dinner at the Guildhall under the watchful eye of Inspector Trehayne, the Prime Minister reluctantly held a small, oddly-attended meeting at Number Ten. The Secretary to the Cabinet was there; so was the Chief Whip, the Minister's wife and Private Secretary, and the junior Minister of Health, who was there because he was also a practising psychiatrist. The meeting was brief, and tragically conclusive. There was an inter-lude while confirmation was obtained from the Yard that the strange episode on the motorway had been cleared up. Two men had been arrested. They had robbed a couple of motorway restaurants and then had turned to a modern version of highway robbery. Infuriating likely cars into stopping by driving close behind them, they then robbed the occupants on deserted stretches of the motorway. The Minister's wife explained about their home telephone having been out of order . . . and how that too had upset her husband enormously. None of them mentioned, because none of them knew about the aftermath of a forgotten incident that took place somewhere in the Troödos Mountains of Cyprus, twenty years earlier, when he as a young second Lieutenant had been hospitalised for some weeks suffering from strain. The Army had never made mention of it at the time; had not the young man been awarded an M.C. for exceptional bravery in wiping out a terrorist group single-handed? In propaganda terms, that he had had a break-down afterwards was an unhelpful matter. In any case, the young man had quickly recovered and his lapse was soon forgotten amid the praise which he reaped for his exploit.

The Prime Minister summed up the conclusions of the meeting. The psychiatrist, who had used a technical name for what the rest called an anxiety complex, explaining that self-doubts often came even to successful men in their forties – a sort of male menopause – had been firmly squashed by the P.M. and told that party loyalties come first. As a very junior minister, the psychiatrist had ambitions, so he agreed at once. The Minister would be taken for . . . go for treatment . . . but not till after the by-elections. Nothing must ruffle the calm before then. Until then, his staff, policeman, Private Secretary and wife would keep a close eye . . . would shield him, be with him, ensure that he did nothing that would cause comment.

During the week following that meeting and the Guildhall dinner, the Minister was never left alone, and he gradually returned to his effective, abrasive self. In his planning for the next Geneva Peace Talks, his Civil Servants had never found him so decisive, so much in control of the situation – and himself. His public opposition to the L.F.G. being allowed to participate in the Peace Talks, was strongly underlined in a well-publicised address to the Foreign Press Association. The P.M. was impressed by the speech. He told the Secretary to the Cabinet that he had been fussing about nothing; the Minister was in full control of himself. As is the nature of Secretaries to the Cabinet, Sir Lloyd accepted the rebuke in silence. The P.M. followed this up with a remark made caustically to the Chief Whip, that he had always thought that the Minister's wife was a bit hysterical; she was of that inbred mixture of fox-hunters, merchant bankers and the Guards that so often led to insanity in the end. She would be taken to the bin before the Minister, he said wisely. That the Minister's wife continued to note that a confusion of anxieties still riled her husband, in consequence counted for little. Lara also noticed, but because she now came to him late at night after the Inspector had gone off duty, she remained a secret part of the Minister's life and could only keep her own counsel.

Inspector Trehayne saw that the strains were still there, but even he was relaxed by the evening of the Economic Advisers dinner. It was held in the roof-top Directors' dining room on the twenty-fourth floor of the Unity Building in the City; the Minister was to make the keynote speech. He was relaxed and confident and even managed to joke with the Inspector as they walked into the pre-dinner reception. Trehayne felt that he could get away with having a gin and tonic even though he was on duty. The Minister would be the last to complain. He stood unobtrusively against a wall, glass in hand, watching the progression of the Minister round the room, shaking hands, smiling, backslapping.

Then everything changed. The Minister was standing, white, shaking. People were looking at him oddly. Trehayne moved over quickly. As he approached, he heard one of the hosts ask the Minister if he was all right. The Minister ignored him, turned and grabbed Trehayne's arm.

'Get me out of here. I saw them. Over by the door,' the Minister whispered.

'Yes, sir. Of course, sir. You'll be all right, sir. A breath of fresh air . . .'

'I tell you, I saw them, Inspector.'

'Let's go out for a bit, sir. Just till dinner begins.' The Inspector gently but firmly led the Minister to the door. The host hovered anxiously.

'I hope you aren't feeling . . .' the man began.

'The Minister will be fine. Just excuse us a moment,' said the Inspector briskly.

He escorted the Minister to the plush, carpeted Directors' washroom, listening to the babble of semi-coherent chatter from his ward. Something about men with their hands above their heads; men surrendering; a young Lieutenant standing between them and their weapons and mowing them down with his machine gun, then throwing their guns across their bodies. 'Armed . . .?' the Minister pleaded. 'Of course they were armed . . .'

'Yes, yes, immediately, Minister. I'll make a full investigation.'

After a quick check inside the washroom, he left the Minister to sluice his face with cold water and went and stood outside the door. Arms folded, guarding against casual interruption, he would stand there until the Minister had regained his control. In Inspector Trehayne's view, his charge was near breaking-point. By-election or no by-election, Prime Minister or no Prime Minister, the Minister would blow his mind before the week was out.

Inspector Trehayne waited a full five minutes and resisted equally all blandishments by hosts who were anxious to get on with the dinner and by fellow diners who had more direct and urgent need of the washroom facilities. After that time, he went back inside.

There was a service entrance to the washroom: a narrow metal door had been carefully blended to match with the expense of the wild silk wallpaper. This door was normally locked. The man and the dark-haired woman entered expertly and silently. The woman, armed with a gun, guarded the main door, outside which the good Inspector stood with arms resolutely folded. The man pushed at the window from which the two security bolts had already been removed. The two had been ready for violence, but the Minister stood transfixed by fear. Grotesque images of life and death in which Lara and a weeping girl on a remote Cyprus mountainside played their subliminal part, flashed through his consciousness and were gone. Then there was nothing. Water from the handbasin, mixed with saliva, trickled down to his chin.

'*Suicide*', screamed the headlines. That a brunette called Lara pestered the police, arguing that the Minister would never have the courage to take his own life, was an incident that rapidly became buried in police files. Equally, Head of Section Nine did not pass on the report from L.F.G. sources that suggested they in some way had assisted in the fulfilment of an old vendetta. After all, everyone knew the truth: the L.F.G. had, almost overnight, begun courting international respectability and consciously shedding their terrorist image. Commentators now believed that they would be invited to the next round of Peace Talks that had been postponed until after the funeral.

Michael Underwood

FINALE

Whenever I have occasion to dip into *Who's Who*, I usually look first to see what the contributor has listed under 'Recreations'. This can often tell one more about the person than all the lines taken up with his accomplishments. It invariably paid me dividends when I was still an estate agent and dealing with important clients. It always helped if I was able to talk to the person concerned about gardening or theatre or sailing or whatever the subject might be. The fact that my own knowledge of it might be minimal mattered far less than that I showed an interest.

Of course, sometimes the failure to mention a particular hobby could prove even more revealing. I recall selling a property for a High Court judge on one occasion. He was a stiff, unbending man without any noticeable sense of humour. 'Walking' and 'Reading' were listed as his unexceptionable recreations. It was only when I visited his house I learned quite by chance that he would pass his winter evenings doing embroidery. His obvious desire to keep this fact secret lowered him still further in my estimation.

But all this is really by the way. What I had been going to say was that, had I ever been invited to contribute an entry to that prestigious volume, I would have headed my list of recreations with 'Opera, especially Wagner'.

I have a passion for Wagner that has taken me to

performances in places as far apart as Moscow and San Francisco, Vienna and Buenos Aires. In fact, since I retired five years ago, most of my travelling has been devoted to his cause, with an annual statutory visit to Bayreuth, the shrine for all Wagnerians.

I ought perhaps to say that my passion is unshared by most of my friends who regard it as an aberration in an otherwise reasonably normal person.

But however strong the lure of Wagner, attendance at his operas can bring hazards of their own. For example, you can find yourself sitting next to someone who fidgets or coughs, or be faced in the foyer by a notice regretting the indisposition of one of the leading singers. These things can, of course, happen at performances of other operas, but with less disastrous effect. And even if you manage to escape these particular hazards, others still lurk, for no composer loaded his singers and musicians, not to mention his producers and stage-hands, with such superhuman difficulties. Even when the singing and orchestral playing are sublime, disaster can still strike. The dragon in *Siegfried* can get inextricably caught up in a piece of scenery, the hero's sword can break in two just after it has been invincibly forged and majestic Valhalla can develop an incurable wobble like a jelly on a vibrating surface. The list is almost inexhaustible.

And recently I was involved in a nightmarish drama that not even a practised Wagnerian has ever envisaged. Death on the stage is one thing, but sudden death in the auditorium is something different altogether, particularly when, to use the police colloquialism, foul play is suspected.

When a few years ago the well-known philanthropist, Sir Julius Meiler, announced that he was proposing to build an opera house in the park of his Oxfordshire home and devote it primarily to an annual festival of

Wagner operas, there was great enthusiasm amongst us devotees, though, inevitably, a vociferous outcry from those who are always ready to advise others how to spend their money, as well as from those who felt that Sir Julius was betraying his part Jewish blood.

But Sir Julius, who had not made his vast fortune by kowtowing to public opinion, went quietly ahead with his plans. He added that as he could no longer travel to Wagner, he would realise an ambition and bring the composer's work to his own doorstep. He employed top men at heaven knows what expense and from his drawing-room window he was able to sit and watch the edifice slowly rise up a quarter of a mile across the parkland.

Even if he never entertained any doubts about the ultimate success of the project, there were many, like myself, who saw it all ending with the old boy's death or in hideous bankruptcy. But neither of these events occurred and six months before the first performances were due to be given, the box office opened.

Needless to say, Sir Julius had himself decided which operas were to be performed and long before the final bricks were laid, conductors, singers and producers had been engaged for the first season. There were to be two cycles of *The Ring* and three performances each of *Parsifal* and *Tristan and Isolde*.

Though, as I say, I had been sceptical about the outcome of the project, I had made up my mind that, if it did come off, I would be there, come hell or high water. Fortunately, I had a contact in the box office manager who was a friend of a friend.

I can still remember my excitement the day my tickets arrived. They were for the second cycle of *The Ring* and for performances of the other two operas. Not even the horror of subsequent events has dimmed my recollection of that sunny June morning when our cheerful postman delivered the self-addressed envelope that had accompanied my application.

There were still three months to go before that fateful performance of *Die Walküre* on Tuesday, 22nd September.

For the non-Wagnerian, I ought to explain that *The Ring* (full title: *Der Ring des Nibelungen*) consists of four operas amounting to about twenty hours of music, if you include the intervals. Wagner believed in giving his fans their money's worth and some of his 'acts' are as long as whole operas by other composers. So far as *The Ring* is concerned, *Das Rheingold*, which is the first, is the shortest. It lasts just under two and a half hours and is performed without an interval. From this, you will gather that stamina is almost as important as love of the music. If you're given to fidgets, you'd better stay at home and listen to recordings.

I had been over to Bargewick Park (Sir Julius Meiler's place) a couple of times before the festival opened. Once to a large and noisy party to which I was invited by my friend, the box office manager, and once for a privately conducted tour of the opera house itself which I had found much more interesting. It wasn't an elegant building to look at, but the acoustics were said to rival those at Bayreuth. Sir Julius had insisted that everything should be subordinated to the acoustics, hence the somewhat functional interior. The seats might be on the hard side, but they were guaranteed not to absorb any of the sound.

I greeted Monday, 21st September with a sense of great exhilaration. It was almost beyond the dream of any Wagnerian that the operas were about to be performed with internationally famous singers in a brand new theatre almost on his own doorstep. Bargewick Park was, in fact, twelve miles from where I lived. The Gods could not have been more beneficent.

Das Rheingold was scheduled to start at half past seven

and I arrived a good hour before that. The car park was already quite full and I made my way to the long bar which ran the length of one side of the building and bought myself a glass of champagne. What else on such an occasion! Almost everyone was in evening dress and the air of expectation was enormous. Wagnerians had flocked from all points of the compass to attend the opening performances.

After a second glass of champagne to put the seal on my mood, I decided to go and claim my seat. I had studied the plan in advance and knew exactly where it was – one from the end of the twelfth row of the stalls.

An elderly man and his arrogant-looking younger companion were already occupying the two seats to the right of mine. They tucked their legs in with a poorly-concealed lack of grace to let me pass, for which I murmured my thanks. Seeing that there were still fifteen minutes to go before the curtain rose, their attitude seemed rather churlish. Wagner may bring us together, but, as I've discovered before, he doesn't necessarily make us love each other.

The seat on my left, which was against the wall, was still empty and I wondered who was to be my neighbour on that side.

A sudden outburst of applause greeted the arrival of Sir Julius Meiler who was wheeled in his chair into a specially prepared space in the centre of the circle.

The house lights were dimming when I became aware of upheaval at the end of our row as a middle-aged woman pushed her way along to the empty seat on my left.

She was obviously hot and bothered and almost fell headlong over the feet of the two men next to me. I stood up to let her past more easily and then held her seat down for her. She murmured profuse thanks and sank back with an audible sigh of relief as those incredible opening chords rose from the orchestra pit, signifying our immediate transportation to the bottom of the Rhine.

It was not long, however, before I became aware of suppressed coughing on my left and I shot her a quick glance to indicate my awareness. Then at the very moment when Alberich the dwarf seized the Rhine-maiden's gold, she began rummaging in her handbag. Recognising the symptoms all too well, I realised that in her rush to arrive on time she had left her cough lozenges at home. She held a tissue to her mouth and tried to clear her throat in silence, which, as everyone knows, is quite impossible. Hastily I reached into my pocket for the throat pastilles I always carry on visits to the opera. I seldom require them myself and am motivated entirely by self-protection.

I passed her the whole tin and she communicated her gratitude by patting my hand.

They obviously did the trick for there were no further disturbances and the performance reached its majestic end with the Gods making their entry into a satisfyingly solid-looking Valhalla.

'Wonderful, wonderful,' she murmured to me several times in the course of the curtain calls which continued for fifteen minutes.

Eventually the house lights came up and we both sat back in our seats temporarily exhausted while the two men on my other side thrust their way out as if they had a last train to catch.

'You enjoyed the performance?' I said to her after the curtain had come down for the last time.

'Enormously. Surely you did, too?'

'Very much. Though wasn't it Ernest Newman who said one'll have to wait till one reaches heaven for the perfect performance of Wagner?'

'If the rest of the cycle is as good as that, it'll be an unnecessary wait as far as I'm concerned,' she said.

I laughed. 'I'll reserve judgment until we've heard more.'

She reached down for her programme which had fallen to the floor and gave a hitch to her shawl which had slipped from one shoulder. 'I do hope I didn't disturb you with my chokes. You saved my life with your cough sweets. I was sure I had some in my bag, but I must have forgotten them in the rush of leaving home. I kept on being held up and thought I was never going to get here. I think I'd have lain down and died if they hadn't let me in.'

'You certainly ran it rather close,' I remarked. 'Don't forget that tomorrow's performance starts at six!'

'My husband'll be at home to see I set off in good time. He was out at a meeting this evening or I'd never have been late. He's one of those punctual people who has never missed a train in his life. I shan't dare tell him I forgot to bring my cough lozenges.' With a laugh she added, 'He regards them as a minimum requirement for sitting through Wagner. But then he's hopelessly unmusical. We have a pact. He lets me come to the opera and I let him go off catching butterflies.'

'He's an entomologist?'

'He's written a book on the subject,' she said with a touch of pride.

As we walked together towards the car park, she told me a bit more about herself. She lived in North Oxford and her husband, who had been a supply officer in the navy, now worked in the bursar's office of one of the colleges.

I estimated her age as being around sixty. She had a pleasant round face and, I suspected, a perennial weight problem.

We reached the car park and were about to part company when she let out an exclamation.

'I've never given you back your cough sweets.' She fumbled with her handbag and promptly dropped it.

'Keep them,' I said, retrieving her bag. 'You may need them tomorrow. And, anyway, I've got more at home.'

With that, I bade her goodnight and went in search of my car.

The next evening I arrived at Bargewick Park soon after five o'clock and once more fortified myself with two glasses of excellent champagne before going to my seat.

I was both surprised and gratified to find Mrs Sharpe already in her place (she had told me her name was Helen Sharpe before we parted company the previous evening).

'See!' she said with a note of triumph. 'I'm not the scatty female you obviously thought I was.

'No problems getting here this evening then?' I said with a smile.

'My husband pushed me out of the house far sooner than was necessary and I've even brought my own cough sweets this time.' She gave me a rueful look. 'But I've just discovered that I've left yours at home. I'm terribly sorry. They were in my other handbag.'

'Don't worry! I've brought a further supply.'

'What a couple of philanthropists you and Sir Julius are! One provides the music, the other the cough sweets,' she said with a merry laugh.

Shortly afterwards, the two men on my right took their seats without so much as a nod or glance in my direction and a few minutes later, the cellos were whipping up the storm music that forms the prelude of the opera.

Act I of *Die Walküre* is one of my favourite parts of the whole *Ring*. It lasts over an hour, but, for me, there is never one flagging second. And when the roles of Siegmund and Sieglinde are sung as gloriously as they were that evening, I quickly became immersed in the music and oblivious of everything else around me. Mrs

Sharpe could have been coughing her head off and I don't believe I'd have noticed.

I turned to her as soon as the curtain came down and was surprised to see her leaning against the wall on her other side in apparent sleep.

It was only when the lights came up and people began to leave the auditorium that I turned back to her. With horror I realised it wasn't sleep that had overcome her, but death.

I must say that the authorities at Bargewick Park were as efficient at removing bodies from the auditorium as they were at putting on an opera. In no time at all, Mrs Sharpe's remains were carried out with the minimum of fuss.

I went off to the bar and had a large brandy to help me recover from the shock of my discovery. When we returned for Act 2, I realised I was more distracted by the empty seat on my left than I had been by the poor woman's coughing the previous evening. My discomfort was compounded by the man on my right who seemed deliberately to turn his shoulder on me. For the first time I glanced round at the occupants of the two seats immediately behind. They were a middle-aged couple and the woman gave me a nervous smile before quickly looking elsewhere.

I have seldom enjoyed anything less than I did those two remaining acts. When the performance was finally over, I decided I ought to go and make myself known to someone in authority. It had only occurred to me toward the end that they might still be trying to identify Mrs Sharpe. I could at least help over that.

Accordingly, I hung back until the theatre was almost empty. Even so, I received a number of curious stares and it suddenly dawned on me that people had taken her to be my wife or, at least, my companion for the evening and were now regarding me as some sort of callous monster.

I had just reached the foyer when a man stepped forward.

'Excuse me, sir, but may I have a word with you for a moment?'

'Of course. Is it about Mrs Sharpe?'

He didn't reply, but led the way to a door marked 'Private'. It was a small office and there was a man inside whom I recognised as the house manager. His photograph appeared in the souvenir programme.

'I believe you're Mr Mason, sir?' the first man said.

'Yes. Charles Mason.' For a second I couldn't think how he knew my name, but then I realised he had obviously found out by checking my seat number against my application form.

'I'm Detective Chief Inspector Jackley,' he said. 'I gather you knew Mrs Sharpe?'

'No, I'm afraid not.'

He frowned. 'But you mentioned her name when I first spoke to you, sir.'

'We'd exchanged names when we left together after last night's performance.'

'You'd not met her previously?'

'I'd never seen her before in my life.'

'I see,' he said, in a tone which clearly implied that he was reserving judgment on every word I uttered.

'If you look at my written application for tickets,' I said slyly, 'you'll see that I'm on my own. I imagine Mrs Sharpe's will show the same. She told me that her husband wasn't at all musical and never accompanied her on these occasions.'

'I see,' Jackley said again in the same faintly disconcerting tone. 'Well, I think that's all for the moment, Mr Mason. Can we reach you, if necessary, at the address given on your ticket application form?'

'Yes, that's my home.'

'Good, then I needn't detain you further.'

I got to the door and paused. 'Did she have a sudden heart attack or something?' I asked.

'We shan't know the cause of death until after the autopsy,' Jackley said, giving me a funny look.

It was only when I was driving home that it occurred to me to wonder what on earth a Detective Chief Inspector would be doing investigating a case of straightforward heart attack.

I spent the next day pottering about the garden trying to take my mind off what had happened, entirely without success. Normally, I would have been eagerly looking forward to *Siegfried* the following night and to the final opera of the cycle, when the whole monumental undertaking reaches its musical and dramatic climactic. It was no use telling myself that there couldn't be a better way of dying, because I kept on remembering Detective Chief Inspector Jackley's intrusion on the scene.

About half past five I went indoors and had a wash. I had just settled down to watch the early evening news on television when a car drew up outside and two men got out. One of them I recognised immediately as Jackley. For a few seconds they stared up at the roof as if searching for some structural fault. Then they advanced up the path. I waited until they had rung the bell before going to open the door.

'Good evening, Mr Mason,' Jackley said. 'I wonder if my colleague and I might come in and have a word with you? Incidentally, this is Detective Sergeant Denham.'

I led the way into the living-room.

'Nice home you have,' Jackley remarked, glancing about him. 'But then it'd be surprising if a retired estate agent couldn't pick himself a plum.' He gave me a small smile.

My ex-profession had certainly *not* appeared on my

application form for opera tickets, so it was obvious that the police had been doing some home-work on me. Moreover, they were ready to let me know the fact. I decided to hold my tongue and oblige them to state their business, which Jackley wasn't long in doing.

'I understand you supplied Mrs Sharpe with some cough lozenges,' he said with a mildly quizzical expression.

'Not last night. It was during the performance the previous evening.'

'That agrees with what Mr Fox and Mr Driver have told us.'

'And who might they be?'

'They occupied the two seats on your right. They saw you pass Mrs Sharpe your tin of cough lozenges.'

'Oh, did they!' I exclaimed in a nettled tone.

'You sound put out,' Jackley said equably. 'I thought you Wagner worshippers were all chums together.'

'There was nothing chummy about those two as far as I was concerned.'

'But you're not denying you handed Mrs Sharpe your lozenges?'

'Of course not. Why should I deny it? And, anyway, so what?'

'Ah, so what, you ask! Well, the answer to that, Mr Mason, is it appears Mrs Sharpe didn't die a natural death, but was poisoned. Murdered by a dose of potassium cyanide. Now that's a poison that acts very rapidly and so the irresistible inference is that she must have ingested it during the actual course of the performance. That's where your cough lozenges become relevant.'

'Oh, my God, that's terrible!' I said, feeling as if the Chief Inspector had given my room a sudden violent spin. 'But it certainly couldn't have been anything to do with the ones I gave her. She left them at home yesterday and brought her own.'

'What makes you say that, Mr Mason?'

'She told me so. Apologised for not returning mine. Said she'd left them in her other bag, the one she'd been carrying the previous evening.'

For a moment, Jackley looked non-plussed. 'She told you that?'

'Yes.'

'When?'

'When we met at our seats yesterday evening.'

'I can't understand why she should have said that,' he remarked in a tone of clear disbelief, 'because it wasn't true.' He reached into his pocket and pulled out a tin which was enclosed in a cellophane envelope. 'Is this the tin you gave her?'

'Yes, that's the sort I buy. Buckland's.'

'We found this tin in her handbag when we were called to Bargewick Park last night. There was also a packet of Coff-Stop lozenges in the bag. Can you explain why she should have lied to you, Mr Mason?'

'I can only repeat what she said to me.'

'Doesn't it strike you as very odd?'

'I don't know enough about the lady to answer that,' I said warily.

'And you still say that you had never met her before?'

'Never.'

'You don't live far apart.'

'Nor do I from a hundred and twenty thousand other people in this area, but I assure you I don't know them all.'

'That's the best you can say?'

'It's all I can say.'

'Do you have a further supply of Buckland's lozenges?'

'Yes.'

'Any objection to handing them over?'

'None.'

'If you tell Sergeant Denham where they are, he can fetch them.

'I'll fetch them myself,' I replied frostily.

'You don't trust the police?' Jackley said with an air of faint amusement.

'It doesn't seem that they trust me.'

'I assure you I'm doing no more than duty requires, Mr Mason. At this stage of an enquiry, it's questions, questions all the way.'

'And I've given you truthful answers.'

'Every answer has to be tested. You say that yours are truthful, but I have to be sure.'

'You can be.'

'But can I?' He fixed me with an intent look. 'It doesn't exactly tally with what Mrs Sharpe told her husband when she arrived home the night before last.' The room seemed to take another violent spin as Jackley went on, 'According to Mr Sharpe, you had considerably upset his wife. You behaved so strangely that she began to wonder if you mightn't be a mental patient. And she became even more apprehensive when you forced your cough lozenges on her.'

'What absolute rubbish! I don't believe for one moment that she ever said anything of the sort. I've never been a mental patient in my life and there was nothing remotely strange about my behaviour. You can ask the couple who were sitting behind us.'

'The fact still remains, Mr Mason, that she did have your tin of Buckland's lozenges in her handbag last night. Are you quite sure she told you she'd left them at home?'

'Absolutely.'

'Ah, well!' he said with a sigh. 'If you'll just let us have your remaining supply, we'll be on our way. I'll doubtless be in touch with you again.'

After their departure, I poured myself a large Scotch and sat down to try and sort out my thoughts. To say

187

that I was in a state of shock was a pathetic understatement. I felt as if my whole world had become unpivoted.

The immediate decision which faced me was whether to attend the performance of *Siegfried* the next evening. If I didn't go, it would be quickly assumed that I was in some way connected with Mrs Sharpe's death. If I did turn up, I was going to be the cynosure of furtive glances and whispered comment, the effect of which not even the power of Wagner's music was likely to erase. Moreover, I kept on recalling that part of the plot involves a character named Mime trying to induce Siegfried to drink a potion of poison. At least, they didn't have cough lozenges in that mythical era, but nevertheless it was hardly conducive to an evening for forgetting one's troubles.

In the event, I did go and found the experience every bit as grim as I had expected. My attendance at *Götterdämmerung* two nights later was not quite as bad, though it was still testing enough. On each occasion I sat staring at the stage with fixed concentration, remaining in my seat during the intervals. Mrs Sharpe's seat was unoccupied at both performances and Messrs Fox and Driver regarded me with even greater disdain than previously.

What should have been exhilarating occasions had turned into a ghastly ordeal.

A week passed before I heard anything further. I scanned the local paper each day, but news of the case was soon reduced to a small item on an inside page to the effect that police enquiries were still continuing into the 'mystery of the opera-goer's death'. Earlier Mr Sharpe was reported as saying there must be a mad poisoner at large who was prepared to strike indiscriminately as nobody could have had the slightest motive for murdering his wife. I took this to be an arrow shot deliberately in my direction.

I had a great urge to call Detective Chief Inspector Jackley, but refrained from doing so as I feared he might misconstrue my interest in his enquiries. I tried to telephone my friend in the box office at Bargewick Park. Three times, in fact. But once he was at a meeting and the other two times I was told he was out, so that, in my slightly paranoid state, I immediately assumed he was trying to avoid me.

All in all, it was the most nerve-wracking and miserable week of my life. By the end, I had almost become a recluse, even finding it an ordeal to be with friends.

I was just sitting down to a lonely cold lunch one day toward the end of the following week when the telephone rang.

'Mr Mason? Detective Chief Inspector Jackley here. Are you going to be home this afternoon?'

'As far as I know,' I said, trying to sound unconcerned and knowing very well that I would be at home.

'Good, I'll drop by about four o'clock.'

His tone had told me nothing and I spent the next three hours in wild speculation about the reason for his visit.

He arrived alone and accepted the offer of a cup of tea, both of which I took to be hopeful signs.

'I think we've got the case just about sewn up,' he said, as I handed him his tea. He gave me a wry smile. 'As far as I was concerned there were only two suspects from the very outset. The husband and you. And the husband was always the more likely. The problem was to establish a motive.'

'And you've been able to do that?'

'Yes.'

'What was it?'

'Oh, the usual. Another woman. A much younger person.'

'Was she involved too?'

He nodded. 'She's a research chemist at one of the

laboratories. It was she who doctored the fatal cough lozenge. All he then had to do was put it amongst the others and wait for his wife to consume it. I gather she sucked them all the time, so he wasn't going to have to wait very long. The only uncertainty was when and where and he made various contingency plans to meet each situation. For instance if she had died at home, he would have immediately destroyed the packet from which it came.'

'He certainly lost no time in setting me up as the fall guy,' I remarked ruefully.

Jackley nodded. 'When she returned home that first evening and told him how you'd offered her your lozenges, he quickly saw his opportunity for diverting suspicion. He not only made sure she took her own the next evening, but reduced the number in the packet so that she was bound to reach the fatal one in the course of the performance. Then, unbeknownst to her, he put your tin of Buckland's lozenges at the bottom of her bag where it would later be found.'

'He's told you all this?'

Jackley smiled. 'Once we picked up the bit of gossip about his association with the girl, we were able to apply pressure in the right place.' He let out a sigh. 'Murderers of his class often fail to foresee how they will react after the event. They envisage themselves as made of steel and discover too late that they're frightened jelly babies.'

'Fortunately for you,' I remarked drily.

'Oh, we have to apply the correct chemistry as well. I believe catalyst is the word. That's us.' He finished his tea and rose. 'Anyway, I thought you'd be interested to hear the outcome.'

'I'm much more than interested. I'm heartily relieved.'

He laughed. 'I'm afraid we shall need you as a witness at the trial.'

'When will that be?'

'Some time next spring I would think.'

'I'm going away in April for about ten days.'

'Not Wagner again?'

I nodded. 'In Vienna.'

He shook his head in mock despair. 'Some folk never learn, do they?'

John Wainwright

I HATE KIDS

I hate kids. Nor is that just a wild generalisation result-
ant upon my present situation. All my life I've hated
kids; noisy, smelly, sticky creatures: that, or precocious
little brats deserving a swift clip across the ear-hole. I do
not subscribe to the school of thought which insists that
kids are 'miniaturised ladies and gentlemen'. The hell
they are! If they're miniaturised anything, they're
miniaturised weapons of total destruction; each one is a
walking menace to the rest of mankind; each one is an
individual part of Armageddon hiding behind a not too
savoury exterior.

And women . . .

A few hours ago I was explaining this to Ted Lacy.

'How,' I said, 'you can tolerate women *and* kids is well
beyond my comprehension.'

'I'm a happily married man.' He grinned that inane
grin of an otherwise sane man who has been conned and
straitjacketed into a situation from which there is no
escape. 'I love my wife.'

'Dare any married man say otherwise?'

'I love my kids.'

'In which case, you're definitely certifiable.'

'If I didn't know you . . .'

'If *you* don't know me, who does?' I challenged.

And (as I knew) there was no answer to that. Lacy is
a detective – a jack – and a very good jack. In my not
totally undistinguished career of crime he has stood me

in the dock five times. No hard feelings, you understand. We like each other. We respect each other. Each of us is from what is commonly called 'the old school'; the 'fair cop school'. Unlike the modern hooliganised breed, I abhor violence of any kind. I have no desire to inflict hurt upon anybody. More important, I have no desire that people should inflict hurt upon me; life is *not* the bowl of cherries the song would have us believe it to be, therefore why make it even *more* uncomfortable?

It was my call, and I took the empty glasses to the bar of the lounge for re-filling. When I returned to our corner table we each tasted the top of the bitter before I sat down to continue the conversation.

Ted said, 'The last one, I'm afraid.'

'The "little woman"?' I mocked, gently.

'No.' He glanced at the lounge clock. 'Actually, there's a new American cops-and-robbers series starting. I'd like to see it.'

'Good God!' For the moment, I thought he was joking.

'I like 'em,' he smiled. 'Very relaxing.'

'All those hair-raising car chases.'

'Good fun.'

'All those guns.'

'It's all make-believe.'

I tasted my beer, then asked, 'Tell me . . . would *you* like to be shot at?'

'Good lord, no.'

'What makes you think the criminal enjoys it?'

'I don't think he does.' He chuckled. 'Jimmy . . . it's not for real.'

'From what I hear it's not far from reality.'

'No.' He shook his head. 'Violence – vicarious violence – it's part of the present-day society.' He smiled, knowingly, then added, 'I won't use a gun. I promise.'

'When?' I asked innocently.

'Next time I nick you.'

I looked suitably shocked, and murmured, 'My dear Edward, didn't I tell you? It's all over. These days I'm an upright citizen.'

'In a pig's ear.'

'Now, that's not nice,' I protested.

'I hope you mean it.' Suddenly he was very serious. 'Because, if you don't . . .'

'I know.' I nodded. I, too, could put on a serious face.

'You're getting too old for a really hefty stretch.'

'Indeed,' I agreed.

'And next time that's what you'll get.'

'If there is a "next time".'

'I hope not . . . for your sake.'

And I believed him. And why not? Wives and kids notwithstanding, Ted Lacy was (still is) a very nice man. A comfortable man with whom to spend an hour or so in the lounge of a public house. A man incapable of bearing grudges. A little dumb, perhaps – but one must make allowances for certain traits found in all policemen – but a man for whom today is the only day of any consequence. Yesterday is a mere memory. Tomorrow is still a dream. Today matters – this particular moment is the only piece of reality available – so why worry?

He left me, and I stayed and drank alone until closing time. I drank very slowly – very moderately – because I required a clear head and as much wit as possible. I also required darkness, and the comfort of the lounge seemed as good a place as any in which to await that darkness.

Meanwhile, I thought great and profound thoughts.

About men like myself and the police, for example. It has long surprised me that some long-haired intellectual had not, as yet, taken the police/criminal relationship as the basis for a thesis. An as yet unexplored aspect of ecology . . . surely? Assuming all men (including women, of course) were honest. No more thieves, no more breakers, no more dips, no more three-card tricksters. No more law-breakers of any kind, in fact. Think of the economic shambles. Think of the sudden rise in unemployment. No more police forces . . . policemen would be superfluous. The lawyers, too, the army of solicitors and barristers we keep in steady employment, what would *they* do. The prisons. The prison officers. The judges, the court officials, the traffic wardens . . . the mind positively boggles!

It can be argued, therefore, that I and my ilk are indispensable. Or, at least, almost so. Without us, there would have been no Patrick Hastings, no Edward Marshall Halls, no Spilsburys; indeed, clear the mind of bias and there can be little doubt that we have done much to make this nation famous. Even great. We are the unsung, unacknowledged (even despised) power-pack vitally necessary to the advance of civilisation.

Why, then, should I excuse my profession? I am a house-breaker. In my own small way I ensure the circulation of money – I help perpetuate what the economists call 'cash flow' – and thus prevent monetary stagnation. I handle only high-quality goods, and those goods are insured – well insured: or if they aren't they should be and the owner can hardly find legitimate cause for complaint in having to pay for a lesson well taught. It follows, therefore, that if I steal I steal from insurance companies; from well-endowed institutions whose profits border upon the obscene.

My profession, although illegal in the strict sense of the word, can in no way be described as immoral.

Happy thoughts. Warm, comforting conclusions which were my companions as I strolled from the public house as dusk deepened into darkness.

As I climbed into my car I chuckled quietly at the

mental vision of Edward. Ted Lacy . . . one of the town's best collar-feelers. Gawping at a television screen; surrounded by howling, nerve-jarring kids; with a wife bawling petty complaints from the kitchen; finding some small degree of escapism in the fictitious antics of make-believe American policemen with a proficiency for wrecking motor cars.

Such an agreeable man, too. It hardly seemed fair.

I drove carefully. Very carefully; one must take basic precautions. For the same reason I zig-zagged around the town, and kept a weather eye on the rear-view mirror. When I was quite sure I wasn't being followed I did another one-for-luck circuit of the town before driving up the ramp of the multi-storeyed car park.

On the third storey I found a gloomy corner, parked, turned off the lights, switched off the engine and waited. One must have patience when engaged in these escapades; there must be an absolute minimum of 'improvisation'. The Golden Rule . . . an hour of care and thoughtful planning can eliminate a year in one of Her Majesty's Prisons.

The van, for example. The van was parked and waiting on the second storey; that, also, had been parked carefully, and only after another round-the-houses trip as a warranty that it was not being followed. I took it for granted that the police knew my car; knew its make, knew its registration number, knew its colour and (at a pinch) knew the mileage on the clock. Or, if not the whole force, at least Edward and those of his colleagues possessing a similar degree of thoroughness. What they didn't know about was the van. Any of the vans. It was my practice to change vans after each successful job; to trade in a moderately well-serviced second-hand van for *another* moderately well-serviced second-hand van. A different set of wheels for each break-in. Simple precautions . . . no more.

I sat in the darkened car for about twenty minutes.

Other cars came and went, their exhausts booming and echoing in the low-ceilinged enclosure. Nobody was standing around. Nobody was strolling from nowhere in particular to nowhere else in particular. I was happy. I was not being tailed.

I locked the car, took the lift to the first storey, then climbed the stairs back to the second storey. Again . . . no echoing footsteps followed me.

I started the van, followed the painted arrows on the floor, passed the exit and returned to my original parking place. No vehicle followed and, again, I was satisfied.

I climbed into the rear of the van, removed my jacket, shoes and trousers and climbed into the track suit. I slipped the rope-soled climbing shoes on to my feet and returned to the driver's seat.

The break-in, proper, was under way.

The target was one of those small-scale country-mansion structures; built by egotists, purchased by idiots and costing the earth to keep even moderately warm and draught-proof in winter. They belong to no particular county, no particular period and, if they have a common denominator, it is an architect who has not yet progressed beyond the child's-building-bricks stage. They are neither handsome nor ugly. They are merely nondescript and (invariably) they stand in their own hundred acres or so of ground with grazing for sheep, a tennis court at the rear and row upon row of windows, one of which *must* be an open invitation to gentlemen like myself.

Almost without exception, their owners flaunt their wealth. The silverware is in every room. Every shelf has its quota of Dresden figurines. Wardrobes bulge with furs. Jewellery is never 'costume'. Each drawer of every dressing-table seems to have its own expensive watch, its gold cuff-links, its diamond-studded tie-pin.

Aladdin's Cave held no more treasure than do these isolated, box-like dwellings of the *nouveau riche* and their own self-esteem generally precludes them from even giving thought to the installation of a safe; it might be misconstrued, by their own kind, as an admission of quasi-poverty . . . that they cannot afford to replace their wealth, should it disappear.

In short, these foolish people are God's gift to men following my own profession.

And, of course, when they holiday they *holiday*! From the general to the particular; this family (for example) are away on some 'island-hopping' cruise in and around the Mediterranean; for a week, now, they have been making themselves an infernal nuisance to pursers, guides, waiters, shopkeepers . . . everybody in fact. I know their kind. They always do. Their holiday continues for another three weeks; the man, his wife and his two kids. And how do I know this? Because *they* have told me. Indirectly, of course; this type of man does not count himself as receiving value for money until he has caused minor havoc at some travel agency; he is happy only when he has reduced the manager to a state of nervous breakdown, and the typists and counter-clerks to the verge of tears. And these people are human. Having suffered such ignominy they seek a shoulder to cry upon . . . and *my* shoulder is always available.

The van was tucked away in a tree-shaded lay-by within fifty yards of the main gate. I'd jog-trotted to the house – seeking what shadow was available from the clumps of rhododendrons and laurels flanking the drive – and I was now examining the windows. There was a near-full-moon and scudding clouds and, for the moment, I needed no other light. I gave the front of the house a mere cursory examination; experience told me that front-facing windows and doors are always far more secure than those at the rear. I moved to the side

of the house; to where fall-pipes and soil-pipes identified the position of bathrooms and toilets. And, to the
accustomed eye, even without the aid of a torch, the
entry-point I was looking for could be identified; that
slightly thicker bar of shadow; the differing angle of the
glass which mirrored an image inconsistent with that of
the other windows.

I pulled the thin, leather gloves over my hands.
Golfing gloves; gloves made to allow a firm grip, without restricting the movement of hands and fingers. I
shinned up the pipes; fall-pipes and soil-pipes are as
negotiable as a builder's ladder to a practised climber
wearing rope-soled shoes. I wedged myself in the
narrow window inset and, for the first time, used the
pencil torch. Easy. Ridiculously easy! The transom
window had a faulty stay. Below the transom window
was a small casement window, with a cockspur fastener.
A quick jerk with the tempered steel 'jemmy' (a
purpose-built tool which started life as a large, top-
grade screwdriver) and the transom window was open.
After that, I merely reached inside and pulled up the
cockspur fastener. I was inside and taking a few deep
breaths within seconds.

The problem at this point in any break-in is the
surfeit of adrenalin. Like 'first-night nerves' it can lead
to foolish mistakes. Indeed, like acting, the 'thrill' is the
ingredient which makes house-breaking worth the
candle; the knowledge that your chosen profession is
not some dreary, nine-to-five, run-of-the-mill occupation; that, in the final analysis, success or failure rests
upon your own shoulders . . . upon your own skill. To
follow the analogy, a prison sentence can be likened to a
play which, despite all efforts, has turned out to be a
flop. Sad. Disappointing. But part of the game and no
real reason to cast your vocation aside. There will be
another play – another break-in – and with it the
success you deserve.

So, having quietened my nerves, and using the torch as little as possible, I sought the linen cupboard.

Why the linen cupboard? Because only a fool – only an amateur – carries with him more than is strictly necessary. The sack with the word 'Swag' stencilled on its side is, of course, a childish joke. But of almost equal ludicrousness is the holdall, the gunny-bag – indeed *anything* – which points an additional clue to the night's activities. For myself, I prefer a pillow-case. Not one taken from one of the beds; its absence is an immediate give-away, whereas one filched from the linen cupboard can sometimes not even be missed.

After that, the bedrooms. Systematically and with speed, but with care. First the wardrobes; many things are tucked away at the back of wardrobes; binoculars, cameras . . . on one occasion a boxed pair of beautifully engraved duelling pistols. Wardrobes are always worth more than a passing glance. After that, the bed; just a lift of the mattress in order to check that nothing of value has been 'hidden' there. Then the various drawers. *All* drawers.

With drawers, the amateur starts at the top and works down; which means he wastes precious seconds closing one drawer before he opens the next. The semi-professional starts at the bottom and works up, thus saving a little time. But the professional (like the amateur) starts at the top but (unlike the amateur) pulls the drawer out, completely, and tips the contents on to the bed. That which is of value is always at the *bottom* of a drawer and, by upsetting the drawer on to the bed, that which is of value is immediately identifiable. The result is a mountain of junk, from which all disposable loot has been removed and, as a bonus, the devil's own job, as far as the owners are concerned, determining what has, and what has not, been stolen. This, in turn, tends to make the insurance people suspicious and the police a little less enthusiastic.

After the drawers came the shelves and the dressing-table tops. Checking in each vase. Opening each box. And within fifteen minutes, my pillow-case was becoming weighty with treasure; treasure for which I already had a buyer; treasure which (hopefully) would not even be missed until the buyer himself had disposed of it. A copybook 'break'. And if the property downstairs equated with the property I'd found in the bedrooms, a life of ease for a few months. A small luxury here and there; an occasional visit to some five-star restaurant; a week or so in London seeing the sights and visiting the shows. Nothing excessive. Nothing too extravagant. Merely a self-assurance that crime, if committed with care, *can* pay . . . and quite handsomely.

I opened a door, flicked the pencil-torch on and off and saw that the room was the bedroom-cum-playroom for the kids. The usual bunk beds; the football and boots in one corner; all the normal junk associated with the so-called 'best years of our lives'. Certain it was there was nothing of value *there*. Another couple of doors; a bathroom and a loo. I decided I'd creamed the upper floor and decided to make my way to the living quarters.

It was a nice night. The moon gave illumination enough for me to walk along the carpeted passage without the help of the torch. I was happy. My step had a distinct spring as I hurried to the head of the stairs . . . then, quite suddenly, I was airborne.

I recall (quite distinctly) hearing the bone of my leg snap; *hearing* it, rather than feeling it. Then almost at the same moment, the nape of my neck came in contact with an edge (a very hard edge) which, at a guess, was travelling at not much less than the speed of sound . . . and after that, nothing.

I returned to the land of the living slowly, painfully and with an almost irresistible desire to vomit. I must have been out for at least two hours; the first grey hint of dawn was there at the windows of the hall. Enough light to see the pillow-case, well beyond my reach. Enough light to see the telephone table about two yards away on my left. Enough light to see the peculiar bend in my left leg, below the knee and well above the ankle. I needed no light at all to feel the pain; at that moment I was sure my leg had snapped off, like a broken pipe-stem.

And, on the face of things, I was there for three more weeks; until the owners of this infernal house hopped their last island and returned home.

The hell I was!

I wormed my way to the telephone table. Slowly, agonisingly, but with that philosophical state of mind which we, of the criminal fraternity, must develop, I reached up, lifted down the telephone and dialled a number.

Edward's voice answered.

'Hello?' He sounded half asleep.

I told him who I was and where I was. I ended, 'You were so right. You won't need a gun, but bring an ambulance.'

He said, 'Why?' but I didn't bother to answer.

I replaced the receiver and as I waited, I wallowed in a great sea of loathing. I gazed across the hall at the blasted skateboard some lunatic child had left at the head of the stairs – the skateboard which some slap-happy mother had overlooked in her urge to start some cockeyed holiday – and, I tell you, I *hated* kids.

David Williams

TREASURE FINDS A MISTRESS

'Books and pencils put away? Desks clear? Hurry up Avril, you're holding up the class. That's it. Now off you all go to Miss Anderson for exercises. Peter, I want to talk to you a minute. Lucy, tell Miss Anderson Peter will be along shortly.'

'Yes, Miss Hardwick.'

The other children trooped from the class-room. Peter Martin, a backward, lonely child waited to be spoken to by the Form Three mistress of Mrs Eastern's Private Junior School (boys and girls, 4 to 8) in the village of Upper Trestle. He was an unprepossessing, bespectacled 7 year old but to Miss Hardwick, an unprepossessing, bespectacled 48 facing the first daunting day of another repellent school year, he was suddenly offering unexpected promise.

She opened the folder on her desk: sixteen crayon submissions hardly distinguishable from what a bunch of baboons might have produced given the same materials.

'Peter, your entry for the "Holiday Secret" competition is very good. Very good indeed,' she lied.

'Thank you Miss Hardwick.' The flicker of pleasure was short-lived. There had to be a catch: there always was. She didn't like him for a start. His Grandmother was the same.

'Did you remember the rules? You didn't show it to

anyone else. Not to Mummy or Daddy. Oh, I forgot, you live with your Grandma don't you?'

'Yes, Miss Hardwick. I didn't show it to anyone' – because no one would have been interested to see it.

'Not to any little friends?'

What friends? Why would he spend all the holidays bird-watching if he'd had anyone to play with, and a fat chance you had bird-watching with only opera-glasses and grown-ups messing about under your hide. He shook his head.

'We don't want *anyone* to see until the exhibition, do we?' He shook his head again. 'And you're sure the lady and gentleman under the.tree were Dr Edwards and Mrs Coptlin-Snag?' She smiled encouragingly. 'By the way, that's Coptlin not Cuppling as you've spelled it.' If he'd been older you could have called that a Freudian slip. 'And you were up the tree?'

'In Dean Copse on the way to Glandon Magna, Miss Hardwick.'

'Quite. And it was just the once you saw what you wrote here.' She glanced down at the inscription which read 'Docter Edwerds and Missis Cuppling Snag li-ing dorn an kissin undur a tree.' What was the point of being a teacher? 'Just the one occasion?'

'No, Miss Hardwick. Every day 'cept Sunday one week.'

'And you watched them every day . . . er, kissing?'

'Kissin' and dressin'. . . an' doin' things. Like on the farm.'

'As on the farm,' she corrected mechanically. 'But you must understand, Peter, that Dr Edwards is a doctor. He could have been examining Mrs Coptlin-Snag.'

'Is Mrs Cupt . . . Coplin . . . is she a doctor too because she was . . .'

'I don't know, Peter. Anyway, it's none of our business and really you shouldn't have been watching

204

like that, and certainly not day after day.' He knew there'd be a catch. 'Was it last week, perhaps, or the week before?'

'Both, Miss Hardwick.'

'I see, Peter.' She gave the drawing a slow, appraising glance then without intending to be enigmatic said, 'On seconds thoughts, I don't think it's quite up to exhibition standard.' He knew it. 'But I'm going to keep it for my special secret collection of promising – very promising – drawings. That means it stays a secret between us, Peter. It also means a very special prize.'

He looked up, eyes opened wide in anticipation. 'Can I have something I want, Miss Hardwick?'

'That depends, Peter.' Inwardly she was pursuing a parallel train of thought. 'It depends what you have in mind – and if you're ready to promise.'

He told her – and he made the promise.

'Yes, in the circumstances, Doctor, my associate and I thought £10,000, or £1,000 a month for a year, whichever suits best – but either way in cash of course. And that will be the end of the matter. You have my word. My bond. My values and standards are of the old fashioned kind. Oh yes.'

She was the last patient of the Friday evening surgery – not a regular patient: she wasn't on his list. He knew her of course. Dammit, she taught his own daughter at the school in the next village.

She had telephoned saying she wanted a second opinion – privately, as a paying patient by appointment and as late as possible. He'd had no reason to refuse her: an extra fee was always acceptable. It wasn't unethical: it just turned out not to be medical either.

'I appreciate you're still newish to the practice, Doctor. Just over a year now isn't it?' She looked around the consulting room. 'You've spent a bit on new equipment I expect. I suppose the private patients

cover it. We wouldn't want to bankrupt you of course.'
She gave a little laugh to accentuate the absurdity of the
notion. 'But Mr Coptlin-Snag being such a rich busi-
nessman – tipped for a Knighthood they say – we
thought his wife would be ready to help pay out of the
er . . . house-keeping. Not that I expect she calls it that.
Probably gets a big allowance to cover her pleasures as
well as essentials and . . . and medical expenses.'

'You understand this is blackmail, Miss Hardwick.
That I could go to the police.'

'Oh yes, doctor, it's a sort of blackmail, but more
protection my associate calls it. For a trifling sum –
well trifling to Mrs Coptlin-Snag – you can take my
word for it, as a lady, your little secret will stay safe,
whereas it could easily have got out. Our sources of
information are impeccable – we have dates, times,
even . . . even pictures. They'll all be destroyed. We
have our expenses too of course, but you won't have to
worry your head about *those*. We're all inclusive, as the
brochures say.

'You won't go to the police of course. They never do
manage to keep it confidential you know – especially
when it's *Doctor* X. So sad for your nice little wife. Even
sadder for Mrs Coptlin-Snag if she had to give up all
that luxury. I gather she's his third wife. So young and
pretty, oh, and athletic too, I believe. And with his
being abroad so much it must be lonely for her. It's no
wonder.' She paused and gave an understanding smile.
'Mark you, they say he's a jealous man. Well with all
that money and responsibility I suppose he's entitled.
You weren't thinking of divorcing Mrs Edwards to
marry Mrs Coptlin-Snag?'

So that was it: the scrawny bitch had it figured right
through to the Sunday newspapers, the Divorce Court,
and the British Medical Association's Disciplinary
Committee.

He was no more ready – emotionally or economically – to break up with Jennifer to marry Marjorie than Marjorie would be to chuck the *dolce vita* and go back to modelling or whatever it was she did to support a struggling GP lumbered with alimony and child maintenance.

In any case, it just wasn't that kind of an affair. It had been a delicious, exciting, uninvolving relationship up to a moment ago: now it had turned sour, sordid and potentially disastrous. Marjorie was his patient. He had known the risk. There'd been nothing he could do short of suddenly telling the Coptlin-Snags to find another doctor with John Coptlin-Snag demanding the reason – or possibly deducing the right one.

Probably Marjorie could find the money. Paradoxically, her husband certainly would if he knew. The Knighthood wasn't moonshine: Marjorie had said it was as good as promised for next June. Coptlin-Snag was much too sold on the probability to let it slip away because of a badly timed scandal. He'd pay, but once he got the title that would be the end of Marjorie. She'd be sent packing in quicker order than previous wives, with no grounds for compensation.

And they'd been so careful.

'Let's see, it's September 21st today, Doctor.' She was consulting a pocket diary. 'You'll need the week to talk things over – to decide whether to pay in full or by instalments. The former would be cheaper, of course, but it's entirely up to the two of you. Shall we say same time next week? Then if it is to be £1,000 a month for the year we can begin as we intend to carry on – 7.30 on the last Friday of the month.' She made a little note in the diary. 'If you need more than the week to raise the whole amount that's all right, but I'll still need the £1,000 next week, with no refund I'm afraid. As I explained, we have our expenses.'

He had a dozen methods for exterminating her right there in the room. 'You won't get away with it . . .'

'Oh, I think I shall, Doctor. And now I must leave you. My associate knows I'm here.' She spoke with deliberation as though she had been reading his thoughts. 'I promised to be home by eight. It's only five minutes coming down to Lower Trestle on my bicycle but it takes rather longer getting back. One doesn't want to be the cause for alarm.'

Miss Hardwick not only survived the journey home but was also still in rude health on a Tuesday afternoon early in the following March as she and her visiting 'associate' sat close together taking tea on the sofa in her living room.

'I'd hoped so much we'd have got it all in one lump this time.' Miss Hardwick sighed. 'The woman could easily have arranged it. Not like the couple in Portsmouth – the ones before last. *She* was only a Captain's wife, but she found the lot in a few days: remember? That was a nicer job too, teaching down there. And it paid off. Twice. I've always loved the seaside. Still, it's helped to move about. Dame schools don't vary much really.' She took the other's unusually soft hand in hers. 'We can't complain, Hilary, can we? What with an ex-Cabinet Minister in Kensington . . .'

'Except we should have asked more. A pervert – and careless with it. To think he once had Departmental responsibility for . . .' Hilary was a bit political.

'Dear one, this is the last, barring windfalls,' Miss Hardwick interrupted. 'Another seven months and we'll have more than enough. With the £1,000 I paid in Saturday the Fund is £65,300. Last time we vowed we'd stop at £70,000. It's enough, truly it is, with our other money – and some to leave for Sam, though why someone perfectly capable of fending alone needs kid glove treatment . . .'

'Yes, Rosey, it's enough,' Hilary put in quickly, not wanting to open old wounds.

'I'm sure we can find what we want near Exeter. The West Country is teeming with antique shops.' Miss Hardwick looked around the room proudly. 'There are enough beautiful things here to get us started. Away. Oh away from it all!'

Her companion agreed. The dream was approaching the time when it could easily become reality. 'I must go.'

They embraced – awkwardly because Hilary had never quite overcome the guilt, while Miss Hardwick liked to express the depth of her passion with an enfold-ing, vice-like grip. Hilary decided she was right: it really was time to get away from it all.

'I'll do it . . . I've said I'll do it.' It was mid-morning three weeks later and Mrs Coptlin-Snag was speaking into her bedside telephone. 'No, I don't want to see you again, not until Friday night, and that'll be the last time – ever.'

When your husband has just been offered a Life Peerage – not a Knighthood but a full-blown Peerage with a formal letter downstairs from Downing Street asking if he'll accept – it's marvellous how the priorities sort themselves out. 'I'll be there at 7.40 . . . all right, if she's always early at the surgery, 7.35 . . . You've told me *exactly* where, three times . . . Just you hope the bloody things fit.'

If only her old mum were still alive. Margie Potts that was, sometime photographic model, film starlet, aquatic nursemaid to a troupe of trained dolphins, hostess on a TV give-away quiz show: Margie Potts, born in the Mile End Road about to become Lady Coptlin-Snag of Glandon – provided the prospective Lord Coptlin-Snag never found out about recent indis-cretions and threw her out on her un-aristocratic ear.

'I told you, I don't want to know about your part . . . and stop saying I can trust you. After this we don't need

to trust each other. We'll have too much on each other.'
She could have added that after Friday she'd have a
whole lot more on him than he'd have on her. 'We just
stick to the times agreed . . . I *know* they're important
. . . Of course it's still just between the two of us. D'you
think I'm crazy? . . . He wouldn't go along with it in a
million years . . . Oh, spare me the crocodile tears.' She
put the phone down.

The still youthful Vice Chairman of Grenwood, Phipps
& Co, London Merchant Bankers, stood at the chancel
steps of St Mary's Church, Upper Trestle, looking at
the new east window. He found it worthy – justifying
the twenty minute drive alone in pelting rain from
Mitchell Stoke where he and his wife were weekend
guests further down the Thames.

Wet Saturdays in the country could be the devil, but
village churches were usually open. It had been an
inspired effort to visit this one to assess a work of art
with the whole place to himself.

'Why, it's Mr Treasure.'

Well, almost to himself: she was a small and virtuous
looking matron, middle fifties, slight figure, incon-
spicuously dressed with timorous voice to match.

'Mrs Paget. It's very good to see you.' He grasped her
hand warmly.

'It's clever of you to remember my name.'

Treasure thought so too. Now he began to recall her
properly: refined, long serving record's clerk. 'Ah,
pillars of the New Issues Department are not forgotten
overnight.'

'It's been nearly three years.'

'Indeed? Time flies. And now you live here.'

'Oh no. My husband, he's a sales representative, was
transferred to the Midlands. Otherwise I'd never have
left the Bank.'

'Of course.' He paused. He had a strong presentiment

that Mrs Paget was summoning the courage to un-
burden. 'Isn't that a lovely window? It was written up
in *Country Life* some time ago. I'd promised myself a
visit . . . Mmm. Mr Paget flourishing, I hope?'

'I came for the funeral.' She seemed not to have taken
in his last enquiry which was as well if it was Mr Paget
who was sorely missing. 'My younger sister. She died
two weeks ago.' So it might have been worse. 'My
husband couldn't get away till later to-day. It's left a lot
on my shoulders. I had to stay for the inquest yesterday.
The funeral was on Wednesday.' There was a break in
her voice. 'I came here to pray for guidance, and hoping
to see the Vicar. Then you came in.'

He registered proper concern while inwardly deplor-
ing that coincidence might pass for divine intervention
and serve to undermine the status of the clergy. 'Was it a
long illness?'

'Suicide.' This time it was solecism: dead centre. 'At
least . . . Balance of her mind disturbed the Coroner
said. But Rosemary wasn't like that, Mr Treasure.'

'I'm sure. Perhaps some very private worry . . .'

'She suffered from vertigo.' Surely not a condition
demanding or justifying the supreme remedy? 'And
then there's all the money.'

There seemed no purpose in continuing this conversation standing shoulder to shoulder at the chancel
steps as though present to be joined together. 'Why
don't we find somewhere to talk properly, Mrs Paget?'

'Oh could we? So kind. Rosemary's cottage is just
along the road. I can make coffee.'

Although smaller than Lower Trestle which it overlooked in the river valley, Upper Trestle's one street
included a finer 14th century church and a 19th century
railway halt besides Mrs Eastern's private school.

Oak Tree Cottage, residence of the late Miss Hardwick, was an unpicturesque, detached dwelling built
in the thirties, half tiled above grey rendering with

a lurching wooden garage to one side. The whole was decently screened from the road by an untrimmed laurel hedge. There was no sign of an oak.

'What a charming room,' said Treasure, suppressing his surprise. The rain had stopped, and leaving his Rolls Royce where it stood, they had walked the 200 yards from the church. Now they were drinking coffee before a log fire in Miss Hardwick's sitting room at the rear of the house. Outside was a sloping garden and a fine view beyond.

'The furniture is mostly Victorian, though I think quite good of its kind,' Mrs Paget offered tentatively. 'Some of it was inherited from our grandfather. I fear I sold my portion for very little years ago, knowing nothing about such things.'

'But your sister wisely hung on. Victorian, yes, but some earlier. The bureau for instance and this delightful sofa table.'

'It was one of Rosemary's ambitions to own an antique shop.'

'Sadly not achieved.'

She nodded. 'It was always the same. Nothing ever came right for her. We weren't close. I blame myself for that. We'd not seen each other for ages. My husband dropped in once or twice – when he was in the area. But she was so . . . so jealous, you see, and later . . . well bitter. She had all the brains while I had . . .'

'The beauty,' he volunteered gallantly if without any conscious conviction.

'The advantages I was going to say. I was five years older. As girls we were moderately well off until my father went bankrupt. Rosemary was denied so many benefits I had already enjoyed – and largely wasted. I could have gone to university if I'd had the brains. Rosemary couldn't go because father couldn't afford it. Men didn't seem to care for her either.' Again there was the look of apology. 'She cared for them though. She was secretly infatuated with my husband – that was before we were engaged.'

'Oh, that's not uncommon surely. A school-girl crush . . .'

'It was more than that, Mr Treasure. The night before our wedding she swallowed a whole bottle of aspirin . . .'

'Oh dear. Pretended suicide.'

'That's right,' she put in gratefully. 'That's really all it was the doctor said at the time . . . Then some years later she was jilted by a very small man. I remember his being small.'

'She didn't . . . ?'

'No. She didn't try to take her life over that. Just became very bitter.'

'Did the first suicide attempt come out at the inquest?'

'I'm afraid so. Of course I was asked if there'd been any previous attempts and I had to admit there'd been the one. I explained the circumstances – that it was more than thirty years ago, that the doctor had said it was only a dramatic gesture . . .'

'But obviously the coroner had to take it into account. Did she leave a note? People often do . . .'

She shook her head. Her eyes were filled with tears.

'And she had no special problems that you knew of?' There was no audible response save for a tiny sob. 'Would it help if you told me what happened?'

Mrs Paget nodded vigorously as she dried her eyes. 'Please forgive me, Mr Treasure. It's all still such a shock.'

'Of course. Just tell me in your own words while I help myself to some more of this delicious coffee.'

'It's only powdered. So kind.' She was sitting on the edge of a sofa, her thumbs kneading the handkerchief held between her palms. 'Rosemary had been to the doctor on the Friday evening – that's a fortnight yesterday. She had an appointment for half past seven. It was a Dr Edwards in Lower Trestle. He wasn't her National Health doctor. The doctor on her Medical Card is in Portsmouth where she lived three years ago. She's been seeing Dr Edwards as a private patient since September. It was about . . . about the change of life.' Mrs Paget swallowed. 'The menopause. He said so at the inquest.'

'That's often a troublesome time,' Treasure put in gently. 'I wonder was she over-anxious?'

'The doctor said no. That she had this regular appointment for a check-up every month as a sort of confidence builder. Oh, she was embarrassed about it all – perhaps being a spinster . . .'

'She might have chosen a lady doctor,' he interrupted, 'particularly as she was paying.'

'You're quite right, Mr Treasure. I said the same thing to my husband. It seems there isn't one in the district.'

'Did the doctor say if she was on any sort of medication?'

'Only a very mild tranquilliser to help her sleep at night.' She shook her head in immediate response to the questioning glance. 'She didn't use them to kill herself. She jumped off the railway bridge into the river.'

Mrs Paget was silent for a moment then continued in a quiet monotone. 'She left the doctor's at twenty to eight. He was seeing her out when the *au pair* girl was sent through to the surgery to say he was wanted on the telephone in the house. She remembered the time. So did the doctor's wife. Their house is on the village street but the surgery's in a separate building at the back. I've been to see. You go in from a little lane at the side. It runs down to the river. There's a landing stage.'

'Rosemary had her bicycle with her. Normally she would have ridden it back up the lane, along the street and up the hill home. It was quite dark of course, and no one saw her, but they think she probably cycled along the tow path to where the viaduct crosses the river – that's about quarter of a mile. You can see it from that window. Even if she'd taken the road it's not likely anyone would have seen her. There's no one about at that time, specially in winter.

'They found the bicycle propped near some steps where the viaduct begins. She must have climbed up and walked along the line until she was over the river. The parapet isn't very high. As she was about to jump one of the express trains to Oxford came through. The driver and his assistant both saw her jump – at 7.58 exactly. They said she seemed to wave.'

'They saw her? Both of them? Did they stop the train?'

'They were very good. They were going very fast but they stopped quite quickly. The young assistant ran all the way back to this side of the river and down to the bank while the guard got to a telephone.

'It was all too late of course. The police found the body an hour later at the weir. It's not far away. She couldn't swim. The river was quite high after all that rain we had – higher than it is now. The current must have been very strong. They found the red top-coat she was wearing next day. It was well below the weir. It came off in the water. The train driver noticed the coat particularly – and the woolly hat she wore. They never found that. The hat.'

Treasure looked puzzled. 'Tell me, had she always suffered from vertigo?'

'Since we were children.'

'So it took special courage to choose that way . . . There was a post mortem?'

'Yes. It seemed so unnecessary. They said she died from drowning – oh, while unconscious.'

'I'm sorry?'

'She hit her head in some way . . . on the bridge, before she went into the water.'

'There were head wounds?'

'Only one. A bad graze. It must have knocked her out. A blessing when you think about it. I've always believed drowning must be a terrible . . .'

'Were the pills mentioned? The tranquillisers.'

'Yes. She'd had two prescriptions filled since the autumn but she hadn't taken any. I'd found the bottles upstairs. They were still full.'

'Perhaps it would have been better . . .' Treasure paused. 'Had the doctor said anything to her that might have especially depressed her?'

'He said no – but then what else would he say? Mind you, he was terribly upset – almost distracted, I thought. It's a big responsibility . . .'

'Which most doctors are very well aware of. My guess is he's telling the truth. It does seem your sister succumbed to a sudden impulse . . .'

'But for what reason, Mr Treasure? She didn't particularly enjoy her work. We always knew that. But she was resigned. The people who saw her that day say she was perfectly normal.' She looked up slowly. 'And then there's the money. She was rich, Mr Treasure, at least by our standards. She was much better off than ever we could have guessed. And it'll all come to me.'

Mrs Paget moved to the bureau, returning with five building society pass-books. She gave them to Treasure.

'On top of what she had in the bank she had accounts with all those societies. See, she's been paying £200 into each of them at the end of every month.'

In fact Miss Hardwick had been doing that only since the previous September. A quick examination of the books showed that apart from entries covering interest there was a three year gap before an earlier pattern of regular depositing – at the rate of £100 a month – could again be traced. There were also some larger deposits recorded still further back in the books.

'Well let's hope she paid all her taxes,' said the banker cheerfully. 'If you're her sole legatee I'm afraid there'll be some liability for capital duties on this lot.' He glanced again at the pass-books and then at those pieces of furniture that had earlier taken his eye. 'D'you suppose she was quietly buying and selling antiques?'

'It's possible. Is that illegal?'

'Good heavens no, but if she was doing it on any sort of scale it may complicate things. You say she owned this house? May I ask, have you found a will?'

'Not yet. I've been to her bank. The manager was very understanding. Apart from the deeds to the house she had nothing deposited there.'

'You've looked for a will here?'

'Not very thoroughly, I'm afraid. I've looked in the bureau. My husband warned me not to get any papers in a muddle before he got here.'

'*You*! You get papers in a muddle, Mrs Paget? I can see I'll have to have a word with your husband.'

She smiled shyly. 'I found the pass-books. They were put out . . .'

'Ready for the monthly paying in.' He had taken out a diary and was cross referring from it to one of the books. 'Yes. Always the last Saturday in the month which would have been the day after she died. Hmm. Well if there is a will it's my guess you'll find it in that desk – probably in a concealed compartment.' In answer to her bewildered look he walked across to the elegant bureau.

It was mahogany with satinwood inlay bandings, four drawers below. A flapped down writing top above revealed a beautifully tooled and balanced figuration of drawers and pigeon holes. Late 18th century, and without doubt there'd be a secret . . .

'Behold the secret compartment,' he cried, after a few moments, withdrawing one of the uprights that separated the horizontal sets of drawers. It was hollow at the rear, providing a deep, long, inch-wide slot. 'You can usually find them if you know the tricks. I learn them from my wife who studies antiques when resting from her labours on the stage.' He smiled. 'No will though, I'm afraid. Only a small desk diary and some children's drawings . . . how extraordinary. You'd better have a look at them.' He shook his head. 'It appears your sister collected juvenile porn!'

Half an hour later Treasure walked the short distance back from the river bank to where he had left his car beside the road on the outskirts of Lower Trestle.

He looked up again at the viaduct which here sprang from the solid embankment to carry the railway across the water. The road turned sharp right: horse-power had a hundred years before deferred to steam at this point and been made to trundle up-hill to a low tunnel under the railway just short of Upper Trestle Halt.

The area between road and river was well screened by trees and bushes. It was possible to drive a car some of the way Treasure had walked – indeed it was clear people did so often – on a rough track that petered out at a clearing near the wooden steps that led up the embankment. A cast iron warning notice erected by order of the Great Western Railway recounted the perils and penalties (maximum fine £5) that waited upon unauthorised persons using the steps, but there was nothing else to stop them.

The steel viaduct with stone piers spanned the river in three stages. Treasure estimated the distance from parapet to water as no more than 40 feet: even so, for the vertiginous . . .

Earlier he had interviewed Dr Edwards. After hearing what Treasure had to say, the increasingly agitated man had eventually broken down and seemed actually relieved to admit he'd been blackmailed by Miss Hardwick, while being equally anxious to prove he'd had nothing to do with her death. While he had no reason to assume anything but suicide, the possibility of foul play being discovered had haunted him for two weeks. If this happened, and if the police learned about the blackmail, obviously he would be a prime suspect.

He had had no communication with Mrs Coptlin-Snag since the school-mistress's death – and precious little for months before that. They had long ceased being lovers. They had been seeing each other only on social or professional occasions – the latter arranged solely so that Marjorie could hand him the lion's share of the money destined for Miss Hardwick.

The doctor had no idea what had become of the £1,000 he had given Miss Hardwick minutes before she died. No, Marjorie hadn't asked for her part back.

Edwards had sought to impress three facts upon Treasure. First, a post-mortem by a forensic pathologist had proved beyond doubt there had been no drugs or poisons in the body. Secondly, it had been Helga, the Edwards' *au pair*, who had finally seen a live Miss Hardwick off the premises that night. Thirdly, for the following critical twenty-five minutes he had been on the telephone in his own living room talking to one of the best known heart surgeons in the world, and most of that time in sight of his wife.

As he wiped tow-path mud from his shoes before stepping into the Rolls the banker admitted again to himself that he had heard less convincing defences from palpably innocent people.

Driving back into the village he passed the public telephone box he had used earlier to speak with the Financial Editor of one of the more respected Sunday newspapers at his office. This long-time friend, amused but incurious, had quickly turned up the information required.

As Treasure had dimly recalled, the third wife of the

man currently regarded as Britain's top salesman had first earned some modest public recognition at the age of 16 as a Junior Diving Champion, had later been involved with performing dolphins, and was now a noted organiser and participant in water ski-ing events at home and abroad.

Half way through the village Treasure turned the car left up the middle road to Upper Trestle and right again half a mile onwards down the long drive to Half Way Farm: Peter Martin's drawing had been signed and addressed.

The place seemed deserted. There was no response to two hammerings on the front door.

'My Gran's out.'

Treasure turned and smiled at the earnest little boy who had materialised in the drive behind him. 'Well, as a matter of fact it's you I've come to meet. It's Peter, isn't it?'

The child nodded, clearly preoccupied with matters weightier than his own identity. 'That's a Rolls Royce Silver Shadow Mark II.' He blew his nose on a crumpled handkerchief. 'It's not a Corniche.'

'No, they're more expensive,' the banker replied, feeling mildly underprivileged. 'D'you want to look around inside?'

'Can I?' The solemn countenance suddenly came alive with a look of unalloyed pleasure. The handkerchief was being used now quickly to polish spectacles.

Treasure had made a friend.

'It's a mystery to us, Mr Treasure, and that's a fact. If you can shed any light Samantha and I . . .' He was a big man, gone to seed. She had said they were the same age but he looked older, worn – and every inch one of life's losers.

'I think I can shed quite a lot, Mr Paget.'

'I showed Hilary the drawings,' put in Mrs Paget.

'All except the one you took with the diary, Mr Treasure. Disgraceful is the only word for them, he said.'

They were in the living room of Oak Tree Cottage. Treasure had just entered. It was his third visit to the house. He made a show of consulting his watch. It was nearly one o'clock. 'I'm afraid there's worse to come, Mrs Paget.' He paused. 'That snack lunch you mentioned. If you could busy yourself in the kitchen . . .'

'Mr Treasure wants to spare your blushes, Sam dear.'

'If you could give us a few minutes. It might be better.' Treasure opened the door for her then closed it firmly. 'It was murder, of course.'

'Oh, my God. The doctor?'

'Your sister-in-law was knocked unconscious by a stone probably moments after she left the surgery. The murderer removed her top coat and woollen hat, then quickly – very quickly – threw her in the river from the landing stage. The current would have floated her to the centre and then under the bridge to the weir. Of course, she'd have drowned long before then. Pathologically the body would have been in the same condition as if she'd jumped from the bridge, hitting her head on the way down.'

'But . . .' Paget made to interrupt.

'I think you'd better hear me out. The murderer next bundled the clothes and the bicycle into an estate car parked in the lane, pocketing a thousand pounds in the process. He drove to the embankment, then down to the steps where his accomplice was waiting with her own car. She put on the hat and coat, probably over a wet-suit. She climbed up to the bridge and simply sat on the parapet till the train came. She jumped when she was sure she'd been seen, and then swam ashore.

'Shedding the coat was unavoidable but should have been a give away. Only a conscious swimmer would

221

have done that. Miss Hardwick was supposed to be neither. It wouldn't have come off in the water of its own accord. The hat was different. Just a marvellous cover-all disguise for hair and face.

'The accomplice was being blackmailed by your sister-in-law.' Paget shook his head in amazement. 'I think she'd been doing it for years – with what she called an associate. But it seems they might have been retiring from the game. At the end of August in her diary she's written "£70,000 and freedom with H". She'd also given a term's notice to her employer.' Though how Peter Martin had gleaned that information Treasure would never know.

'H of course is Miss Hardwick's associate – a quite frequent visitor here after dark according to dates and times in the diary. He's also her murderer.' Paget had slowly paled: beads of sweat had formed on his forehead. 'His accomplice, Mrs Coptlin-Snag, he contacted for the first time quite recently. He told her who he was and a cock-and-bull story about being an unwilling collaborator. He said Miss Hardwick meant to go on extorting money after the first lot was paid, and how he intended to atone by arranging a "suicide" if Mrs Coptlin-Snag would help – something she's confessed she was very against doing.'

'She's a liar. It was partly her idea.'

Treasure was perfectly ready to accept Paget's blurted assertion since most of what the banker had just been saying had been pure supposition: he'd had no contact with Mrs Coptlin-Snag.

For a moment there was silence between the two men. Then Paget seemed to relax. He shrugged his shoulders. 'What's the use? You seem to know it all. I should have come for those drawings and the bloody diary. I knew where they were. Safe enough I thought . . . It wasn't for the money. I know it'll sound like it was with Sam getting it all . . . I gave that woman the last thousand back . . . Honest to God it was the promise . . .'

'To leave your wife and go off with her sister?'

'I couldn't do it to Sam, but Rosey would've gone spare if I hadn't. After all those years looking forward – to nothing else. You've got to understand . . . It sounds mad. I probably am mad, but it seemed the best way out. And that stuck-up cow gave me away.'

'Not really. You were under observation in the doctor's lane. There's a picture of you putting the bike in your car – with the licence number clearly visible. The car you've got in the garage outside' – the car Treasure had seen on his first return to the cottage an hour before, making him turn about and telephone the police to meet him.

'But how could anyone've taken a picture? There was nobody. Why haven't they told . . .'

'There was a reason, Mr Paget' – reason why a small boy would not in any normal circumstance show his secret Easter holiday drawings to anyone except Miss Hardwick, even after he knew she was dead. He'd made a promise he'd give up his prize if ever he told about his summer holiday entry – and he never would have if the man with the Rolls Royce hadn't had it with him. He'd not have shown his new drawings either except the man said he'd sort of taken over the competition judging from Miss Hardwick.

Peter had drawn the picture – the one the new judge especially liked – from his attic bedroom window. The lane was dead opposite. It wasn't a very good picture – not good enough to win the camera Miss Hardwick had said might be the *next* special prize. You could see it was a bike going into a car. You could also see the car number. Peter had smiled about that: four-eyes some of them called him.

'There's a Detective Inspector Wadkin in a car out-side, Mr Paget. I think I'd better bring him in now, don't you? Would you like me to have a word with your wife afterwards?'

Paget nodded. 'So it was a photograph that gave me away.'

'Oh no,' Treasure answered evenly. 'Really it was Miss Hardwick. And it's a drawing not a photograph, made by a young bird-watcher using binoculars she gave him as a special prize. They're night glasses actually. Very powerful.'